POLTERGEIST

COVEN: BOOK 9

DAVID NETH

DN Publishing

This book is a work of fiction. Names, characters, businesses, organizations, places, events, and incidents are the product of the author's imagination or are used fictitiously. Any resemblance to actual persons, living or dead, events, or locales is entirely coincidental.

Poltergeist

Coven, Book 9

Copyright © 2022 by David Neth

Batavia, NY

www.DavidNethBooks.com

ISBN: 978-1-945336-28-7
First Edition

Subscribe to the author's newsletter for updates and exclusive content:
DavidNethBooks.com/Newsletter

Follow the author at:
www.facebook.com/DavidNethBooks

ALSO BY DAVID NETH

COVEN
HARPY
SIREN
VALKYRIE
SHAPESHIFTER
SORCERER
WITCH (SHORT STORY)
ENCHANTRESS
ORACLE
TRICKSTER
POLTERGEIST
HEX (SHORT STORY)
WITCH HUNTER
DEMON (SHORT STORY)

UNDER THE MOON
THE FULL MOON
THE HARVEST MOON
THE BLOOD MOON
THE CRESCENT MOON
THE BLUE MOON

THE ART OF MAGIC

FUSE
ORIGIN
OMERTÁ
OBLIVION

HEAT
BLACK MAGNET
DUST STORM
THE GATEKEEPER

STANDALONE
ALL I EVER WANTED

CHAPTER 1

- OCTOBER 1934 -

Henry Powell sat on a bench at the playground in Gridley Park across from his school. The crunchy leaves blew across the grass as passersby tucked their hands deeper into their coats against the chilly breeze.

The joy of that after school feeling was lost on Henry. He had been given strict instructions to come right home after school let out, but still he lingered. As he watched groups of other kids, he swung his feet on the bench and thought about how he would rather be anywhere but home.

He wasn't welcome there.

He didn't want to stay in school, either. Many of the friends he had started grammar school with had left to go work for their families. Henry had only managed to stay in school because his grandfather had left them their house when he died, and it was fully paid for since he was the one who had built it. No need for Henry to work to bring money home for the family. At least, that's what his mother argued whenever his father tried to bring up the topic.

After several minutes of sitting on the park bench, he decided he couldn't put off going home any longer. If it got much later, his father would be waiting and would know that he didn't come right home. With a deep sigh, he got to his feet and proceeded down the street toward home.

When Henry finally made it back, he sat on the front steps of his house. Even before he entered, he could hear his parents arguing inside.

"...you let the kid do whatever he wants!" his father shouted. "He needs to learn discipline!"

"He needs to be a kid!" his mother shouted back. "What are you doing? That's my mother's—*Ivan!*"

Glass shattered.

"Do you know how much that cost?" she asked. "It's irreplaceable!"

"Go make your kid work like everyone else's kids and maybe then we can afford to buy another!"

"You only broke it because it was mine! What if I had poured your booze down the drain? Or broken your rocker?"

"You wouldn't dare!"

Henry could hear the distinct sounds of his father hitting

his mother. Of her collapsing to the floor. The silence was worse than the arguing. At least if they were arguing, he wasn't hitting her. Not usually, at least.

Rising to his feet, Henry rushed inside. Sure enough, his mother lay on the floor, cradling her cheek while his father stood over her, watching her struggle.

"And where the hell have you been, boy?" his father asked him. "School let out half an hour ago! Did that stupid little head of yours get lost?"

"No," Henry said quietly.

"Then what took you so long?" Suddenly, Henry was face-to-face with the full force of his father's rage. He had been here before—several times, actually.

Henry stammered. He wanted to tell his father to go away. To leave him and his mother alone and never talk to them again. But he couldn't. His father wasn't going anywhere. And even if he did, there was no way they could survive. His father was the only one who worked in the household. He brought home the money that they used to go to the market. He paid the bills that kept them in their house. He earned enough so that Henry didn't have to go to work himself.

Before Henry could respond to his father, his mother stepped in between them, putting her son behind her.

"Leave him alone," she said. "Let the boy have some peace and quiet in this house for once in his life!"

Henry watched as his father studied the two of them. There

wasn't a trace of love in his eyes. Only obligation. He was stuck with these people and he certainly wasn't happy about it. Henry felt the same way about him.

Finally, he turned and stalked off to the front door. "I'm going to the bar."

Both mother and son watched as he left. Neither of them dared move until he was out of sight.

"Are you okay?" Henry asked his mother.

She waved it off. "Nothing that some ice can't fix." She dropped to her knees and took his face in her hands, offering a sad smile even as she winced at the pain. "What about you, sweetie? How are you? How was your day?"

Henry shrugged. "When's he coming back?"

His mother shook her head. "I don't know, dear. Probably not for a while, which means it's you and me for dinner. I was thinking about making spaghetti. I know it's your favorite. What do you think about that?"

Henry's mind was still on his father. He cast a look toward the front door and said, "I'm scared."

His mother's face drooped to a frown as she pulled him in for a tight hug. "I know, honey. But I'll always protect you. Remember that."

Henry smiled and kissed his mother on the cheek—the side that wasn't rapidly swelling.

"What do you say after dinner we listen to some music and relax in the living room before bed?" she suggested. "Just the two of us. We'll have fun together."

Henry nodded and grinned for his mother's benefit. "Okay."

As his mother went into the kitchen to fix their food, Henry stood in picture window and hoped that his father would stay gone. It was a hope he knew would never come.

CHAPTER 2

- OCTOBER 1989 -

Kathy checked her watch as she waited for her second bus to arrive. She had just gotten out of work and was meeting Steven's mother at her house to finalize plans for Samantha's baby shower in two days.

Tucking her hands deeper into her pockets, Kathy braced herself against the wind. It was almost the end of October so the weather had turned. She hadn't noticed how cold it had gotten because she had been in the warm office all day.

Dr. Newberg had hired her to take over for Trisha as a receptionist back in June. So far she enjoyed having the steady paycheck and a reason to leave the house each day that didn't result in even more work needing to be done when she came home. But, she could already feel that the nine-to-five routine was weighing on her.

The second bus arrived and Kathy stepped on, dropping her fare in before taking her seat. She sat near the front. The bus ride wouldn't be long—if the weather wasn't so cold, she would've just walked the rest of the way after getting off at the first stop. As it was, her newfound financial security allowed her to take an extra bus ride if it meant staying warmer for a few more minutes.

By time Kathy arrived at Mary's house, she had already braced herself for overly friendly smiles, subtle jabs, and an argumentative tone. She knew the drill because they had met a couple times already. Just like Samantha and Steven's wedding earlier that year, Mary wanted to have a huge elegant party. Kathy knew her sister would only want something small and intimate, possibly even at someone's house.

"Kathy! Hello dear! Come on in." Mary waved her in with a smile. Kathy was grateful to get out of the damp, chilly air.

"How've you been?" Kathy pulled off her coat and added it to the closet by the door.

"Just lovely, dear," she said quickly before jumping right into her first crisis of the meeting. "I've been thinking about the schedule we've committed to for Saturday." She led Kathy inside with an arm around her. At the table, there were already papers and invitations and menus that the two of them had gone over extensively during previous visits.

"Did the caterers confirm?"

"Oh yes, that's all taken care of." Mary took a seat at the table and reached for her reading glasses. "And we've already had everyone RSVP, so we'll have a full house at the golf club."

The shower was going to be at the Lawrence Park Golf Club, since Mary's brother was a member and was able to get them the reservation for a discount. The cost was still kind of steep for Kathy's budget, but she agreed in order to appease Mary. Sometimes it was better to do that than to waste the energy arguing your point.

"So what's the issue then?" Kathy took the seat beside her.

"Well, with the brunch, the opening of the gifts, and taking pictures, I'm not sure how many of these games of yours we'll be able to get to."

"You're saying you don't think we'll be able to do them at all?" Kathy had already narrowed down the list of games to only three. And she tried to only list ones that would fit in with Mary's standards. Oh, and something that Samantha would enjoy. Funny how through all of this planning, the person they were celebrating sometimes had been forgotten.

Mary rocked her head back and forth, studying the schedule in front of her. "We'll have to see if there's time."

"I'd like to make time for them."

She chuckled. "Oh honey, you can't *schedule* fun."

"Well, we need to give our guests something to *do*," Kathy said. "I'm sure Sam isn't going to want everyone gawking at her all day."

Mary rolled her eyes. "Yes, I'm well aware of her stance on people touching her belly."

Kathy decided to let it slide. That had been a whole separate argument between Samantha and Mary, who thought it was appropriate to rub Samantha's stomach without warning whenever they saw each other.

"I think the games will be the perfect distraction so that Samantha doesn't have to swat away hands the whole time," Kathy said. "We're doing this for her. I want her to enjoy it."

Mary huffed. "Well okay then. I suppose we can cut the photos a little short, but that still only gives us twenty minutes."

Kathy took the schedule from Mary and reached for a nearby pen. "Okay. Well, we can get rid of dessert time. We can just serve them at the same time as the rest of brunch and let people take what they want. That'll save us another half an hour, which leaves almost a full hour for the games." She passed it back to Mary, who looked under her glasses at it.

"Yes, well, I suppose that could work. But you're going to have to call the caterer to tell them about the change!"

"Not a problem. I think it'll be a lot of fun!"

"Oh, I do too," Mary said with the first genuine smile Kathy had seen that day. "I just hope that everyone dresses appropriately. Make sure you wear something nice, dear. Do you have anything that'll work?"

Biting her tongue, Kathy said, "Yes, I have several options to choose from."

Mary looked her up and down. "You have been dressing more grown-up lately."

"I'm working at a doctor's office now."

"That's right. I think Samantha mentioned that the last time we all had dinner. You dropped out of college for it?"

Kathy flashed a smile in an effort to hold in her anger at her sister. "Not for this job, no. But yes, I'm no longer in school."

Samantha hadn't been happy that Kathy had dropped out of college. Kathy thought that blow would be softened by the fact that she had a job at the doctor's office lined up, but Samantha still wanted her sister to follow "the plan." Kathy didn't think that Samantha would take their disagreement out to other people, though. Least of all, Mary.

"Anyway," Mary said, "I think it'll be a splendid day. A nice, formal event that we can remember fondly later."

"Not too formal," Kathy reminded her.

"Yes, yes. I remember their wedding at the *fire hall*." She made a face. "And thank you for asking me to plan it with you, dear. I've very much enjoyed being a part of it."

Kathy had only asked her because Steven thought it would be nice to include his mother. And Kathy didn't disagree, but working with Mary took patience. She was just grateful that the baby shower was almost here and gone so that she could be done working so closely with Mary.

"You're very welcome," Kathy said with a smile. "Is there anything else you wanted to discuss?

"I think we've thought of everything," Mary said. "Remember to call the caterer and notify them of the change with the desserts."

"Yes, I will." Looking again at her watch, Kathy rose to her feet. "I have to get going. I have a date."

"Oh? Will we be planning another baby shower soon? After the wedding, of course."

Kathy laughed nervously. "Not exactly. This is just the first date. I've only met the guy once. So we'll see how tonight goes."

"Just remember not to do anything stupid, dear."

CHAPTER 3

The house smelled musty and dank. Like an old garage. Every floorboard creaked, except the ones that had rotted through. There were some beautiful leaded windows on the first floor, but many other windows had been boarded up throughout the years. In several corners there were piles of leaves and garbage, indicating that the house hadn't been completely sealed from critters and squatters.

"This is…" Samantha paused, one hand on her belly as she looked around and searched for the word to use.

"It needs a lot of work," Steven said pointedly.

"Well yes," their realtor, Rupert, said with a nod of his head. "But you said you were looking for a fixer-upper."

"I guess I just didn't realize it would need this

much…um…*fixing-up.*" Samantha was still in awe at how dilapidated this house was. It looked beautiful outside. A little rough, but nothing that they couldn't handle. Inside was…well, it was too much for them.

"Just keep an open mind and look around," Rupert said. "There are three bedrooms upstairs, a full bath upstairs as well." He pointed toward the back of the house. "The previous owners started to put in a half bath off the kitchen, but I think they got in over their head with renovations and stopped part of the way through."

"How long ago was that?" Steven asked. "It looks like it's been sitting empty for a while."

Again, Rupert nodded. "It's been vacant for a long time, yes. *But!* Think of this as your opportunity to bring life back to this house. You know, this used to be a family home. Back when this was built, these houses held generations of families. Think of the holidays and celebrations and the *life* that happened here. I'd hate to see all of that history wasted if it ends up on the city's demolition list."

Samantha nodded. He had a point, even if she could see right through his sales pitch. She had agreed to look at older homes with character and history because that's what she loved about her own house. With the baby coming, she was convinced that she and Steven needed their own place. And maybe borrowing someone else's history wouldn't be so bad. Maybe she could learn to love an old house that hadn't always belonged to her family.

"Think about it," Rupert went on. "You could finish off the bathroom down here. The hardwoods would look nice once you refinished them."

"And replaced a few," Steven added.

Rupert nodded. "And the light reflecting through these windows would be breathtaking, especially on a Sunday morning when you're sipping your coffee on the couch, watching the leaves change on the gorgeous mature trees along the street. And Gridley Park is just around the corner. This really is a very nice neighborhood. I'm sure you'll get to know all the neighbors in no time!"

Steven leaned toward Samantha and said, "He's really trying to sell us on this place."

She smirked back. "What do you think?"

"I think it'd take a lot of work, but we could do it," he said. "We'd have to fix the floors, work on any structural issues with the foundation, check the roof, that kind of stuff. After that we can do the pretty stuff."

"And we're going to do all of this in two months before the baby's born?"

Rupert scoffed, but offered nothing else. He stepped to the front window and looked out, pretending not to listen.

"If we decide to buy it, the sale of this house wouldn't even go through before the baby comes," Steven explained. "This would have to be over the next year."

Samantha looked around. She tried to imagine spending the next year working on a house while also taking care of a newborn. Oh, and maintaining her full-time job and her duties as a witch.

But it was more than that. Despite it's history and neighborhood location—both things she had wanted in the search for a new house—the house gave Samantha a bad feeling. Like something bad had happened here. She wasn't sure if that was the current state of the house, her pregnancy, or her witch intuition warning her to leave, but the whole place was sending out bad vibes.

"You don't seem like you like it," Steven said.

"Keep in mind that it's dreary out today," Rupert butt in. "When it's the summer time and the sun's shining full force, this place will look great!"

"Do you mind if we have a minute to discuss?" Steven asked.

"No, that's okay," Samantha said. "Let's see the rest of the house. We can talk about it more at home."

Rupert waited until Steven turned to him, as if signaling to go ahead.

"All right then," he said with a smile. "Let's head upstairs and look at the bedrooms!"

The upstairs was small. The ceilings were low—although Rupert suggested they vaulted them to give them more headspace. The bedrooms were also small. The "master" was only slightly bigger than the two other rooms and the bathroom left much to be desired. Tile pieces were falling off the walls. The floors were rotting from dripping water lines before they had been disconnected by the city. Not to mention the fact that there was only a tub and an outdated toilet that likely wouldn't meet modern code enforcement standards. Samantha was just grateful that squatters or critters didn't leave any excrement "surprises."

Back downstairs, Rupert led them to the kitchen.

"Now, you might want to consider taking this wall down between these two rooms," he suggested. "I'm not sure if it's structural so you'd have to have that checked out before you did anything, but wouldn't it look nice to have everything open? And all the natural light would just flood in from all the windows! Remember, many of them are still boarded up."

Samantha was only half listening. Her attention was on the basement door. It made her uneasy. Some sort of negative energy radiated from there and she wanted to get as far away as possible.

"Right here we have the half bath I told you about before." Rupert indicated a small room off the back porch addition. "You can really customize that however you want. It's a clean slate!"

"This kitchen actually doesn't look half bad," Steven commented. "It's pretty big, which I guess is nice because we'd have to put a dining table in here too."

Rupert nodded. "Just update the appliances, give everything

a good cleaning and a coat of paint, and you should be all set."

Even Samantha had to agree that the kitchen was in decent shape. She could almost smell the home-cooked meals that had once been prepared here. As she looked around at the cabinets, her eyes kept flickering back to the basement.

What happened down there? she wondered.

"So the utilities have been cut off by the city?" Steven asked.

Rupert nodded. "Yes, so the house hasn't been winterized in…a while."

"Do you mind if I take a look and see what kind of damage there is?"

"Steven!" Samantha blurted as he made a move toward the basement door.

Both men looked at her with confused looks.

"What's the matter?" he asked.

She looked between the two of them. Steven would understand her concerns—or at least respect them. She was too embarrassed to share her fears in front of Rupert as well.

"Nothing," she muttered. "Just…be careful. You don't know what's down there."

He pulled a flashlight from his jacket pocket and clicked it on. "I'll keep an eye out. Don't worry. You should stay up here, though. I don't want you breathing in any fumes or anything that might be trapped down there."

I wouldn't dream of going down there, she thought to herself, but simply nodded.

Poltergeist

When the two men disappeared down the stairs, Samantha suddenly felt isolated. She heard scratching coming from somewhere. She turned to try to follow the noise, but the more she moved, the more the sound seemed to drift to somewhere new.

It's fine. You're fine. Just relax. It's an old house. There are probably squirrels living in the walls.

Turning to the kitchen cabinets, she idly opened up each one. They were all empty, some still smelling of cinnamon or olive oil or basil. The cabinet on the end, however, had several recipes taped on the inside of the cabinet door.

"Edith's meatloaf."

"Cindy's pecan pie."

"Martha's sauce."

Samantha smiled. This was the kind of history she wanted in an old house. Even though it wasn't hers, she liked the idea of living somewhere that had been a family home before. Somewhere that had been filled with love and life, only to experience it all again with Samantha's own family. She still preferred that to be the house she grew up in, but unless Kathy moved out—and Samantha wasn't about to kick her out of her own house—then she and Steven needed to get their own place. That's what it ultimately came down to.

Samantha noticed something at the back of the cabinet. Stretching up to her tiptoes, she reached for it and pulled it toward her.

A family stared back at her. Three people posed for the photograph. The father had a stern brow and a mean look. The mother had a tense smile. And the little boy just looked sad.

This was the type of thing that Samantha would ordinarily love to have in an old house, but it just gave her the chills. Why did these people look so miserable? Was this the family that had lived here? What actually happened in this house?

Suddenly, a rush of wind hit Samantha out of nowhere. She dropped the frame to the floor as the gust pushed her back several feet.

And just as quickly as it came, it was gone.

"Sam!" Steven called from the basement. "You okay?"

She didn't respond, too shaken by what had happened. It felt like something supernatural, but she didn't feel any different. Had she just imagined it?

"Sam!" Steven called again when he made it to the top of the stairs. Rupert wasn't far behind. "What happened?"

"I—I tripped," she stammered. "Dropped the frame."

Rupert stepped up and picked up the photograph. He turned it upside down to let the broken glass fall to the floor, then used his foot to brush it against the base of the lower cabinets.

"Hmm," he said. "I wonder if this is the family that lived here."

"That's what I thought too," she said.

Steven eyed her another moment, then turned to look at the

picture. "That's kind of neat."

"So!" Samantha said, a little louder than she had intended. "How's everything look downstairs?"

"Old," Steven said. "Outdated. Everything probably needs to be replaced."

"Sounds expensive," she said.

"I'm sorry, Rupert." He stepped to the basement door to close it. "We're going to have to look at our budget and—what's this?" He pointed to the back of the basement door.

Rupert walked up and examined it with him.

"There's scratches," Steven said.

Samantha remained glued to the floor where she was. There was no way she was going anywhere near that basement. All she wanted to do was leave.

"Yes, it appears that way," Rupert said.

"There are full-on *gouges* in the door!"

"Perhaps it was from a dog locked in the basement," he said. "Or an animal got in since it's been abandoned. A basement door like that? That's a simple replacement."

"Everything just keeps adding up in this house, though," Steven muttered as he closed the door. "This is going to cost a small fortune to get up to snuff."

"Yes, well, I suppose that's something to consider," Rupert murmured. Then, more jovially, "Anyway, what do you think? Now that you've seen the whole house?"

Husband and wife looked at each other. Finally,

Samantha shook her head.

"I don't like it," she said. "It makes me feel uncomfortable."

Steven nodded. "It's a big job and I would love to see it restored, but I don't think we're the ones to do it."

Rupert sighed heavily. "Well, that's fair enough."

"Thank you for your time," Steven added. "Maybe you can find us another house that doesn't need so much work."

The realtor led them to the door, his spirit clearly deflated. "I'll see what I can do. In the meantime, if you spot any houses you'd like to look at, just give me a call and I'll set it up for you."

They bid their goodbyes to Rupert and climbed into their car. The whole way home, Samantha still felt the chill from the house deep in her bones.

CHAPTER 4

Kathy gave Jeff a side hug when she met him on the sidewalk in front of the pub restaurant downtown. She had had enough time to go home, change, and borrow Samantha's car before meeting Jeff. It was not the way she ordinarily liked to get ready for dates, but she worked a nine-to-five job now. This was her new normal.

"Hey you," he said with a crooked smile. He wore a flannel shirt tucked into his faded jeans and white sneakers. His blond hair was combed back out of his face, held there by some soft of hair product. "I'm so glad we finally got to do this."

"Yeah, I'm looking forward to it," she said. In truth, it had only been about a week since they had first decided to go out formally. That had also been how long they had known each other.

Their meeting wasn't what Kathy would call romantic, even if it was pretty typical for how she had met a lot of guys lately. They had run into each other ordering drinks at the bar last weekend when she was out with Trisha. He paid for her cocktail from across the room, so she went back to the bar and made sure he had a drink special delivered in front of his friends. She thought it'd embarrass him, but he loved it and used that as an excuse to come to her table and ask her out.

Inside, they got a table under the neon lights of the bar, and examined the menus.

"Have you ever been here before?" she asked.

"Once or twice. I'm not really a bar scene kind of guy—last weekend notwithstanding."

She laughed. "I don't go out too much myself, although my sister would say otherwise. At most, like once a month. And only with my one friend. We have a couple drinks and then head home when it starts to get rowdy. But I've never been here. Is the food good?"

He nodded. "It's decent. Bar food, mostly, but it's pretty good."

Kathy scanned the menu. Most of the options were burgers, mac and cheese, or pub pretzels. There was also the option of a fish fry on Fridays or three different types of salad. She opted for one of those. The last thing she needed was burger greased dripping down her fingers on a first date.

Jeff took a sip of his water and leaned back in his chair. "So tell me more about yourself."

"What do you want to know?"

"Where you work, what you do for fun, what you still want to do…that kind of stuff."

She raised an eyebrow. "My hopes and dreams?"

"Only if you're willing to share." He offered that crooked smile again.

"Well, I work as a receptionist at a doctor's office," she started. "I just started there in June and I really like it."

"Is that what you went to school for?"

She chuckled. "Not at all! Honestly, who knows what they want to do, right?"

He shrugged.

"Oh, so you've got it all figured out for yourself?" she asked. "What is it you do, then?"

"I work for a law firm—but I'm *not* a lawyer."

"You said that with every bit of conviction you could muster," she said with a grin. "So what is it you *do* do if you're not a lawyer?"

"Mostly paperwork stuff," he said. "I draft reports, mail things out, call up clients."

"So basically…a receptionist."

"A receptionist greets people," he said. "I just do the paperwork."

"So a secretary?"

He slumped his shoulders. "Okay okay. I get it."

"I'm sorry," she said. "I didn't mean to rag on your job. But I'm guessing this isn't your final resting place? Where would you ideally like to work?"

Jeff offered another sheepish look. "I *want* to be a lawyer."

She threw up her arms and feigned exasperation. "You just made it sound like being a lawyer was the worst thing in the world!"

"I did not!"

Kathy gave him a look.

"Okay maybe, but that's only because the lawyers at the office make it clear where I stand. And it's *not* with them."

"That's terrible they make you feel like that. Are you going to law school?"

"Working my way there," he said with a nod. "I'm trying to save up enough money so I don't have to take on any loans."

"I get that."

"I just feel like I'm falling behind because I'm already thirty and I haven't gotten settled into a career yet."

Kathy's face lit up. "You're *thirty*?"

"Yeah…" he said slowly. "Why? How old are you?"

"Twenty-two."

"Oh."

"Does that weird you out?" she asked. "The age difference?"

"No. Does it weird *you* out?"

She shook her head. "Actually, I kind of like it."

"Oh yeah?"

"I'm tired of dating boys my age only to hope that they mature. It's a breath of fresh air to date someone who isn't just going to play games with me."

Jeff was certainly not the first guy she'd dated since she and Jeremy broke up at the start of the summer. She had much more free time after this breakup and she was determined to play the field. Most guys only lasted a few dates, if that. Nothing substantial. But it was enough for her. For the time being, at least.

And she wasn't against dating someone long-term if the perfect guy fell into her lap. She just needed to find him first.

"Sounds like you've had a bad dating history," he said.

"Not bad, really—and not something I want to talk about on a first date," she said. "We should be getting to know each other. Not the people we've dated."

"Right," he said with a nod. "So what about you? Is a receptionist where you wanted to end up?"

"Not at all."

"So how did you end up here?"

She shrugged. "I needed something steady. I want to start pulling my weight financially. I live with my sister and her husband. And they're expecting."

"Oh boy. Doesn't that get awkward? Living with your sister's family?"

Kathy gave him a confused look. She hadn't thought of it that way. "It's not like I moved in with her and her husband. We lived together and then she got married and her husband moved in, and now they're going to have a baby. She just kind of started her own family while I still lived there."

"And you're all okay with that arrangement?"

She shrugged. "I guess. Well, my brother-in-law gets frustrated when he wants alone time with Samantha, but usually I take the hint and leave the house for a bit to give them a night in."

"Well, I'm just saying that if I were in your shoes, I'd want to get my own place."

Another thing she hadn't really given much thought to before. Samantha was starting her own family. She would soon be taking over the house with the baby anyway. Kathy really just needed a small space for herself. And maybe with the baby in the house, she wouldn't find living at home so normal anymore.

Maybe getting her own place wasn't such a bad thing.

CHAPTER 5

- OCTOBER 1934 -

Henry knew his Saturday wasn't going to be relaxing. They never were. Every weekend there was always a long list of chores to do around the house, usually set by his father. Sometimes, Henry would be working all day. Other times, it was only until his father stumbled off to the bar. Even then, the work was expected to be done whenever his father sobered up.

The morning had been spent by going to the market with his parents. It was the harvest season, so the market was busy. Henry and his mother walked home with overstuffed bags of groceries from the farmers out in the country. His father had opted to go to the bar after the market.

Even in his father's absence, Henry spent his afternoon cutting the grass and cleaning up the clippings and the fallen leaves from the yard and the sidewalk. As the sun shifted and began to give signs that the day was coming to an end, his mother came out onto the porch when he was just about done sweeping up the sidewalk.

"The lawn looks good, sweetie," she told him.

"Thank you."

"You've been working hard today."

"I have that list of chores," he said. "I still have some firewood to chop up in the backyard."

His mother shook her head. "No. You've worked hard enough today. The firewood can wait until tomorrow."

"But tomorrow's Sunday." It was the only day of the week that they rested, usually after church. Sometimes, though, Henry found himself sneaking up to his room to read or work on homework for school. If his father caught him doing that, he'd be in trouble.

It wasn't so much that Henry's father wanted to honor the sacred Sunday by not working. It was that he liked rules. And the more rules that existed, the more there were to be broken. And the more that could be broken, the more he could dole out punishment.

So Henry had to be really careful.

"And according to the paper it's not supposed to be cold for another week," Henry's mother said. "We still have some time to split the wood. Besides, we still have a small pile from last year. So I think you should go out back and play for a little while before dinner."

"Are you sure?"

POLTERGEIST

She gave him a warm smile. "Yes, dear. I'm very sure. You're still a child. And children should play."

He looked down at the sidewalk. "But I'm not quite done here."

"I'll finish up," she said. "You go play."

Henry hesitated, but his mother came down the steps and took the broom from him. Slowly, he walked along the narrow stretch between houses to the backyard.

Under the porch, there was a soccer ball. Henry had found it on the street on his way home from school a few weeks ago. He had to sneak it home so his father didn't see and stash it where he couldn't find it. The ball was a little deflated, but it kicked around okay.

Henry always dreamed of playing on a team. Of having friends in his teammates. Having people cheer for him on the sidelines. Feeling a sense of accomplishment that he had done something to cheer for.

But that wasn't his reality. So he settled for playing by himself in the backyard.

The fun didn't last long. Even from the back, he heard his father's voice at the front.

"What are you doing?" he asked Henry's mother.

"Sweeping the grass," she said.

"Why isn't the boy doing it?"

"Because I gave him a break."

"Who said he could have a break?"

Henry stashed the ball back under the porch and quietly stepped toward the door. If he could make it inside and start working on the dishes or some other housework, maybe that would appease his father. Make it so that the inevitable punishments weren't so bad.

When he stepped back into the house, however, he knew it was too late. His father had just stepped into the kitchen. The two stared at each other, sizing the other up.

Then Henry's mother stepped in behind him and said, "Don't blame him! He wanted to keep working, but I told him not to."

"Is the firewood chopped?"

Henry stood frozen in fear, staring at his father.

In his silence, his father rushed forward, grabbed Henry by the wrist, and shook him so hard his body slammed against the wall.

"Answer me, boy!"

Henry shook his head feverishly, trying not to react to the growing ache in his head from hitting the wall. "N-no. It's not."

"Ivan, don't hurt him!" his mother warned from the doorway. "Let him go!"

"So you thought you'd relax when there's still work to do?" His father ignored his wife and shook Henry's arm again. "Who do you think is going to pick up the slack? You don't see me taking breaks, do you?"

Henry wanted desperately to point out that his father had

spent most of the afternoon at the bar, but he knew that would only result in harsher punishment. Instead, he shook his head.

His father released him and pointed outside. "So get out there and start chopping! I want that whole pile stacked before you come in. I don't care if it takes you all night."

"Ivan, let him do it tomorrow."

Spinning around, Henry's father waved an accusatory finger at his wife. "You shut your mouth! I'm not done with you!"

The room fell into silence. Henry stood frozen, afraid to leave his parents alone together. Afraid of what his father might do to her.

"Well, boy? What are you waiting for? Go on and get!"

Henry exchanged looks between his parents.

"It's okay, sweetie," his mother said. "I'll save some dinner for you when you're done."

With that, Henry opened the door and stepped out, even though he knew what was coming. Before he had even swung the axe the first time, he could hear his father beating his mother.

CHAPTER 6

Did you even read the directions?" Samantha waved the forgotten folded piece of paper toward her husband.

"I've got them right here, Sam." Steven sat on the floor, pieces of the crib they had just bought surrounded him.

Samantha took a seat in the rocking chair in the corner, one hand possessively over her belly. "You've been at this for a while and it doesn't look like you've accomplished much."

"Did you come in here to nag or to help?"

"I'm just saying, the pieces are labeled for a reason. Not to mention, use common sense. What is the crib supposed to look like?"

"Yes, I know what a crib is supposed to look like, *dear.*"

"So why haven't you gotten anything done?"

"I was laying out the pieces first so I don't have to keep stopping to open things up."

Samantha looked around at everything scattered all over the floor. "Looks to me like you just made a mess."

"Would you leave me alone? Man, you've been cranky today."

She rolled her eyes. The last several times they had argued over the past couple months, Steven had blamed her attitude on her shifting hormones and not on any of his own behavior.

"You know," he went on, "we still have a couple months until the baby comes. This can wait."

"No, it can't," she said. "I want it set up before the shower on Saturday so when we bring home the gifts, we can just put everything away where it belongs. I don't want come home from the shower and just dump things. This isn't going to turn into a junk room again."

"And who says we need to put it all away immediately? Can't we take a minute to look at everything?"

"I don't want things laying around when the baby comes."

"Who said things will be laying around?"

She shot him a look. "I know you. You're not always the cleanest. Besides—" She gestured dramatically to everything laid out on the floor.

"This isn't a mess," he insisted. "It's a *process*. And who said the way you do things is the right way?"

"At least we're not tripping over things in this house."

"Because half of my things are still in storage."

"Are you still complaining about that? I never said you had to keep your things there!"

"And where am I supposed to put it all, Sam?"

Downstairs, the front door opened and then quickly closed. Kathy must've come home.

"Just leave me alone," he said. "Go down and talk to your sister."

She groaned. Things weren't great between her and her sister, either. Samantha was still resentful of the fact that Kathy decided to throw out their whole plan to chance some secretary job. If she had stuck it out with college, Samantha knew Kathy could become a big-shot at any number of companies in the area.

But her sister didn't look much beyond the present.

"Clearly nothing's going to get done if you stay here," Steven added. "I'm tired of bickering with you about this. Just let me work in peace."

"And back downstairs I go," she grumbled. Using the arms on the rocker to haul herself to her feet, she stepped to the door and muttered under her breath, "You carry a bowling ball in your belly for nine months and see how you like moving."

Clutching the handrails on both sides, Samantha slowly made her way down the stairs, one step at a time. She noted that each floorboard creaked louder than normal with her extra weight.

When she made it to the kitchen, she plopped at the kitchen table. Kathy was at the stove, fixing herself a cup of tea.

"I'm surprised you're still up," Kathy said.

"I wanted to get the baby's room straightened before Saturday. Steven's up there now putting the crib together and *apparently* I was no help."

Kathy smiled. "I'm making tea. Do you want some?"

"Nah, that *would* keep me up all night. But you could grab me the Oreos. They're in the cupboard above the fridge—Steven doesn't ever go in there."

Smirking to herself, Kathy reached up and retrieved the cookies and handed them to her sister. "Since when do you allow these in the house?"

"It's what I've been craving." Since Samantha did most of the grocery shopping, she only bought healthy foods. Several years ago it had been because they couldn't afford junk food. Now it was because healthier food gave them more energy and kept them more alert, which they often found themselves needing at a moment's notice. "Can you get me the jelly, too, please? And a spoon?"

"A spoon? Are you going to eat it straight out of the jar? That's a lot of sugar." Kathy opened the fridge and grabbed the jar of grape jelly. She pulled open a drawer and retrieved a spoon.

"Cravings, Kathy. Wait until you're pregnant and then talk to me about sugar." Samantha popped open the top of the jelly, dipped the spoon in, and then grabbed an Oreo and used it to scoop up the jelly on the spoon. She popped it in her mouth and moaned with delight. "That does it! This is exactly what I wanted."

The little sister made a face. "Gross."

"Don't talk to me about the food I eat," Samantha snapped. "Now that you decided to work full time, you can go out and buy anything you want to eat yourself."

"I was curious how you were going to slip that into the conversation," Kathy said with an eye roll.

Samantha munched on her Oreos and didn't say anything else. She knew it had been a low-blow. A bitch move. She had been a major one on more than one occasion to both Steven and Kathy. Even now that she was working full time, Kathy didn't make as much as Samantha did, which was a subject of self-conscience on Kathy's part. Of course, if the younger sister had listened to Samantha and stayed in school, she probably could get a well-paying job after she was done.

Until Kathy came to her senses, Samantha's quips were all she had. And the hormones didn't help, either.

The kettle began to whistle and Kathy turned the stove off.

"How was your date?" Samantha asked around a mouthful of cookies. It was the olive branch they both needed. Bad decisions or not, they were still sisters.

Kathy perked up. "Great, actually! He's older, more mature."

"How much older?"

"Thirty."

Samantha rocked her head back and forth then reached for another cookie. "Just be careful with that."

"He's a gentleman," Kathy assured her. "He works at a law firm, trying to save up money to go to law school."

The older sister made a face, then shoved another jelly-dipped cookie in her mouth. "Who likes lawyers? They're boring and snobby and—"

"Can't be anymore boring than an accountant."

They exchanged glances. "Touché."

"He seems to have his life together," Kathy went on.

Samantha swallowed, then waved the spoon at her sister. "Good. You're going to need someone stable with a college education." She couldn't help herself.

Kathy rolled her eyes and turned back to her tea.

"I'm just saying, we had a plan," the older sister went on. "One that would've set you up for something great."

"I wasn't happy."

"That was only temporary."

"I need to make choices that are good for me and my wellbeing."

"That's all I'm thinking about too," Samantha said. "It just seems like you took the easy way out and quit."

Another sigh. "Can we just drop it?"

"What? I'm just trying to prevent you from ruining your life."

"You're trying to prevent me from *living* my life."

Samantha rolled her eyes. "It doesn't hurt to have some responsibility in your life. Some life goals. You were working toward something. And you threw it all away like a spoiled brat."

Kathy raised her eyebrows and stared at her sister. "I cannot believe you just said that."

"What?" Samantha asked again.

Kathy ignored her and left the room.

CHAPTER 7

It was the scratches that woke Steven up at first. They invaded his dreams to the point where it didn't make sense, only for him to realize that he was asleep and that the noise was coming from somewhere in their bedroom.

When he opened his eyes, however, he couldn't place the sound. It was as if it were coming from all over.

Could it be mice? he wondered. *Or bats?* There was no telling what kind of animals had made nests in this old house.

What was most pressing, however, was his sudden stuffy nose. He hoped he wasn't getting sick.

With Samantha asleep beside him, he tossed back his side of the covers and got out of bed. In the darkness, he shuffled into the hall, but something made him stop.

Downstairs, he heard the sound of the TV playing. He had watched it for a bit before heading up to bed, but he was sure he had turned it off.

Hadn't he?

Forgetting his stuffy nose for the moment, he stepped down the stairs, cringing as each floorboard creaked loudly in the night. He paused after several steps and listened, hoping that Samantha hadn't woken up. When he was satisfied that she hadn't, he pressed on.

The glow from the TV was the only thing that filled the living room. Strange, considering that all of the lights were off. Steven looked toward the kitchen, wondering if Kathy had decided on a midnight snack and some late-night television, but the lights in the kitchen were off too.

"Is anybody here?" he asked, feeling silly immediately after the words left his mouth. What if there was someone really was there? Why would they turn on the TV? And what would he do to them, clad in his underwear? He had left his robe hanging on the back of the bedroom door.

He switched off the TV and cast the house into darkness and silence. Listening carefully, he tried to notice any other notices that shouldn't have been there. Even the scratching seemed to have stopped. Worse, the silence that he had wanted seemed to be more bothersome than the TV.

Deciding that he needed to just go back to bed, Steven made his way back up the stairs. This time, he was grateful for the creaks on the staircase. The noise gave him comfort that he didn't realize he was craving.

Up in the hallway, he started back to the bedroom before remembering that he had been on his way to the bathroom to blow his nose before the TV distracted him.

Stepping into the darkened bathroom, he grabbed a tissue and gave a good blow. Something didn't feel right and he looked down in the tissue and noticed something dark and sticky in the Kleenex.

Flicking on the bathroom light, he paused momentarily to let his eyes adjust before examining the contents of the tissue again. He blinked and did a double take, straining his eyes to open wider in the harsh light. Another moment passed as his brain tried to make sense at what he saw.

Blood.

Turning to the mirror, he again squinted at the light, but saw enough that he grew more concerned. The blood ran down his nose toward his chin.

"Sam!" he called.

"Shh!" she berated from the hall. "You're going to wake the whole house up. Lucky for you, this kid thinks my bladder's a pillow so I was already up." She held her back with one hand and stepped into the bathroom, stopping only when she saw her husband's face. "What happened to you?"

"I don't know."

She reached up and took his face in her hands, tilting his

head from side to side for a better look. "Did you bump your nose on something downstairs? I heard you go down there."

"The TV was on. But I didn't hit anything." He tasted the blood in his mouth now and leaned forward to keep it from draining down his throat. A droplet dripped down as he did.

"Ugh." She pointed to the toilet. "Sit. Let me look at you."

Dutifully, he sat as she grabbed a wet wash cloth and dabbed away the blood from his nose.

"Did you forget to turn the TV off before you came up?" she asked as she cleaned him up.

"No. I remember turning it off."

"Well, obviously *someone* left it on and I went to bed before you." She sighed and studied his nose. "It doesn't look like it's still bleeding. Didn't you taste any blood?"

"Not at first. Now I do."

"Weird," she murmured. "But it's been getting drier with the colder weather. Make sure you drink more water the next few days to stay hydrated."

"Yes, dear."

Samantha smirked and took on a nasally voice. "I'll get you all cleaned up, sweetie, and then it's back to bed for you."

He chuckled, then said seriously, "You're going to be a great mom."

"I sure hope so. It's too late to turn back now." She went back to the sink to rinse the wash cloth, before returning to Steven to finish cleaning him. "I'm surprised you didn't grab your bathrobe. You're practically naked without it."

"I thought I was just blowing my nose. I didn't expect to have to go downstairs. Or sit here for a while." He rubbed his arms and felt goosebumps prickle up and down. "I am a little chilly."

"Well, I'm almost done." She wiped his chin, then turned his head to look for anymore blood. "And if you hadn't left the TV on, you wouldn't have had to go downstairs."

"I didn't—"

"Sit still. I don't want this to get all over the bedspread. We'd never get it out. And when you go back to bed, make sure you sit up. If your nose starts to bleed again, I don't want you choking on it."

"Yes, dear."

She smiled again, then swatted at him. "All right, you're all set. Now get up so I can take care of business in peace and get myself back to bed. Sheesh, this kid is driving me nuts with the somersaults tonight."

Steven stood and left the bathroom, closing the door behind him to give his wife privacy. In the bedroom, he propped up his pillows and slipped back into bed, grateful to be warm again.

As he lay back, however, he felt a sore spot on his back. He adjusted a few times, but settled once Samantha walked back into the room. He didn't want to disturb her if she was having a restless night. Besides, the pain in his back was probably some kink that would work itself out overnight.

Samantha lay beside him, wrapping one arm over him. He kissed the top of her head and then fell back asleep within minutes.

CHAPTER 8

Kathy lay awake, unable to sleep. She heard Steven get up, then Samantha. She heard them talking in the bathroom, but she couldn't make out exactly what they had been talking about. Then she heard the two of them each go back to bed.

And there Kathy lay. Her mind ran wild with the thought that Jeff had put into her head at dinner.

If I were in your shoes, I'd want to get my own place.

There were definitely benefits. She would have privacy. Samantha and Steven would have privacy, especially when the baby came. Plus, Kathy could actually afford her own place now that she had a steady, full-time job.

Best of all, though, was that Kathy wouldn't have to listen to her sister's attempts to control her life anymore. The snide comments about going to college or following "the plan" would be gone, replaced by questions like, "What have you been up to?" or "How are you doing?" or "Do you want to hang out this weekend?"

Of course, that also led to some negatives to being on her own. She'd be *on her own*.

Alone.

Her relationship with Samantha would have to be more deliberate—they'd have to plan when to see each other instead of running into each other as they came and went. Kathy would also have to go to the grocery store, pay her own bills, pay attention to how well the mechanicals of a house were running. All things that Samantha—or Steven—currently kept tabs on.

All of those things Kathy knew she could learn on her own, but it was still a little scary. In the illusion the trickster had put her in back in May, Kathy had a nice apartment. Granted, she had a husband who may have helped with the big things, but everything else Kathy had seemed to manage on her own. Obviously, that had been an illusion and Kathy knew that she didn't have a husband or children, but that would only make living on her own easier because she wouldn't have to manage anyone else.

And that illusion apartment had been nice. It was a loft, very bright and roomy. The decor was a little bland, but that could be changed. Maybe there was a nice loft apartment that she could find that would have enough character or appeal for her liking. Maybe downtown or further up State Street. She would have to look in the paper in the morning. Hell, if she wasn't sleeping now, maybe she could go down to the kitchen and—

Thoughts of her future apartment came to an abrupt end when she heard scratches along the walls. Her eyes darted across the room in the darkness, trying to find the source, but the scratches seemed to be coming from all over.

Tossing the covers back, Kathy stepped to the window to look at the tree branch that used to hang over her window. Last winter, it would scrape against the glass in bad storms, so they had it trimmed back in the summer. Now, there was nothing there to scratch. Besides, the noises weren't coming from the window. It was definitely from the interior walls.

Somewhere.

She followed the sound, pressing her ear against the wall, maneuvering around furniture, decorations, and other obstacles. After traveling most of the room, she still couldn't find the source—and yet the scratching persisted.

"Maybe the vent," she murmured to herself.

When she had first moved into this room after Samantha had taken their father's old bedroom, Kathy had had a particularly frightening night when the one heating vent kept hissing. They later found out it was a clogged duct and the hissing sound was the air slipping by the clog. Even equipped with that knowledge, to this day, that same duct still freaked her out sometimes.

Braving her irrational fears, Kathy got down on her hands and knees and inspected the vent in the darkness. When she got closer she discovered that the air wasn't even blowing.

Yet the scratching continued.

Sitting back on her heels, she looked around the room. She resisted turning a lamp on. That would only make her feel crazy. It was one thing to crawl around your bedroom in the middle of the night in the dark. It was another thing to do it with the lights on. Only psychopaths were wide awake with the lights on at this hour.

Hopefully that's not what this is, she thought to herself. *A psychopath.*

She looked around, trying to figure out where the scratches could be coming from. Finally, she settled on the final frontier of her bedroom: the closet.

When this had been Samantha's room, their father cornered a bat in this closet. Apparently the memory of that still scared Kathy.

The house had history—much of it was now coming back to Kathy.

She opened the door a crack and listened. Then opened it wider and listened some more.

Nothing.

What the hell? she wondered. Turning back to her

bedroom, she listened again.

Nothing. No sound, other than the wind pushing around fallen leaves outside. The scratching had stopped.

With one last attempt at finding the source of the scratching, Kathy opened her bedroom door and stuck her head out into the hallway. Maybe Samantha or Steven had gotten up again—or maybe they both hadn't gone back to bed like she had thought they did.

But the hallway was quiet too.

Shaking her head, Kathy turned to return to her bedroom but jumped as the clock radio beside her bed suddenly blared to life. Michael Stipe, of R.E.M., suddenly erupted in the quiet, demanding that the listener stand.

Kathy raced over to the clock and fumbled in the darkness to try to turn it off.

Is it always this loud? she wondered.

When she finally got it shut off, she slunk back down on her bed. Her heart raced from the excitement. Then, her next thought was: *How did that even turn on?*

Even with everything she had seen as a witch, the unexplained sometimes still freaked her out. And the fact that she had heard the scratching and then the radio—both of which were now absolutely silent—weighed heavy on her mind.

Feeling a little crazy for having searched her entire room in the middle of the night only to come up empty, Kathy lay back in her bed and slipped under the covers.

You need to clear your head, she told herself. *Cool it with the imagination right now and just relax. You'll regret not sleeping in the morning.*

Without any further noises to distract her, Kathy fell back asleep and didn't wake again until morning.

CHAPTER 9

- OCTOBER 1934 -

She was gone.

Henry's mother was dead. The official cause was complications from a seizure, but Henry knew what it really was.

His father.

Before the incident that took Henry's mother—his only protector—there had been no history of seizures at all. It came suddenly, out of the blue. The doctors claimed that was normal. Sometimes, healthy people had seizures so severe that they died. But Henry knew differently.

Right before his mother had the seizure, his parents had been arguing. As always, Henry's father sent him to his room so he wouldn't see what abuse was happening.

But Henry knew.

He always knew.

After a few hits, he could hear the panic in his father's voice.

"Get up," he had said. Then, "Helen? Helen, come on. This won't—*Helen!*"

Henry had rushed downstairs when he had heard her head slamming against the hardwood. Meanwhile, his father stood over her and stared, dumbfounded. Henry did his best to keep his mother's head still as she erupted in convulsions, but she was seizing so much that he wasn't able to keep a good grip on her. Not to mention the head blows she had taken at the hands of his father.

Henry's father finally called an ambulance and rushed her to the hospital. Not surprisingly, he made Henry stay back to "watch the house." The whole time they were gone, all Henry could do was worry.

And then his father finally came home very early the next morning.

Alone. Without a word spoken of what had happened.

Henry wanted to know, but he didn't dare ask. He couldn't stand to hear the words uttered from his father's lips. The ones that would no doubt be followed closely by a lame explanation and a plea to keep quiet about the argument.

It wasn't until later that day that he had confirmed what had happened to his mother. The neighbor across the street brought over a turkey casserole to offer her condolences. Henry had to ask her where his mother was and how she was doing to get any real answer.

At that point he already knew, but he wanted someone to be brave enough to say it to him.

But to hear the actual words, "Your mother has passed away, I'm afraid." That shook him to his core.

Worse, Henry wished he had cried. Wished he had mourned his mother—the only one who truly loved him. But he didn't.

Even as he sat in the funeral home, hugging strangers who offered more condolences and empty promises to help, Henry didn't feel anything. He was numb. It was as if his mother's death had broken something in him that was irreversible. He was never going to be the same.

Henry stared blankly at the men and women dressed in formal black attire. Many of them he had never met. All of them saying how great his mother had been.

Like they knew her.

Like they cared.

Like they didn't go around pretending like her husband *wasn't* beating her up nearly every night.

They were selfish people who only cared about *appearing* sympathetic. None of them actually wanted to help in any real way.

What snapped Henry out of his daze was when his father approached, put his arm around him, and smiled at a perfect stranger.

"Yes, its just the two of us now," he said. "It'll be hard, but we'll manage. The boys!"

The stranger smiled politely.

Henry glared up at his father and his act. Everything about him he despised. His touch. His fake smile. His lies.

Henry couldn't imagine what life would be like now that his mother was gone. She had been his person. His protector. His cheerleader. His role model. His best friend.

His everything.

And now she was gone. And he didn't know what he was going to do.

But in all the uncertainty about his future, there was one thing Henry was absolutely sure of as he stood there in the receiving line: he hated his father.

CHAPTER 10

Samantha knocked on the bathroom door and stepped in while her husband was showering.

"It's just me," she said when she entered. "I just want to brush my teeth."

"I'm almost done," he said over the water. "Unless you want to join me?"

She rolled her eyes as she picked up her brush. "Easy. I have enough to worry about today and being late to work is not one of them." She started brushing and muttered around her toothbrush, "I just noticed you finished the crib. It looks nice. Thanks for putting it together."

"You're welcome," he said. "I got a lot more done after you left."

"Ha. Ha."

"Hey, do you want to go to lunch today?" He turned off the shower and reached outside the curtain for his towel.

"Sure, I'd like that."

Ever since they hit the third trimester mark in her pregnancy, she and Steven had been trying to spend as much time alone together as possible. Samantha had been reading parenting books and she was concerned that their marriage would be strained once the baby came when they would both be exhausted and not tending to themselves in the same way they were used to. She wanted a good, solid marriage before the baby came so they would be more in-sync to help each other out once the baby was born. She wasn't sure Steven bought into her theory, but he was at least open to more lunch dates.

Steven pushed open the curtain and stepped out of the shower with the towel around his waist. "Do you have any places in mind?"

Samantha stepped back as he reached across the sink for his own toothbrush. The question he had just asked slipped from her mind as she noticed his back.

"Where did you get all these bruises from?"

"What bruises?"

She reached up and touched one in particular that felt more like a welt than a bruise.

Steven winced at her touch, then turned to try to see his back in the mirror. "Oh!"

"It looks like someone punched you or something. What happened?"

Steven stared over his shoulder in the mirror. "I have no idea. You know, I felt something last night when I went back to bed, but I just thought it was sore muscles or something."

"Sore from what? It's not like you work out."

Steven shot her a look through the mirror.

She spit in the sink, rinsed her toothbrush, and put it away before turning back to him. "Well, I'm just saying the truth, dear. Here, let me see." She gently touched his shoulders and moved him to inspect his injuries better. "Steven, you're a mess! First the nosebleed last night and now these bruises. Did you get into a fight in your sleep? Was it the boogeyman? I saw the Andersons had him out down the street."

"Very funny. I must've hit my back on something. And the nosebleed I think was just the air. But I woke up this morning without any issues up in here—" He waved in front of his face. "—so I think I'm good with that. It must've been a fluke thing."

"Just be careful." She kissed his shoulder, then reached for the mouthwash. "I don't want you to come home from work with a broken bone or whatever else you'll have next."

"I promise to be careful." He reached for his bathrobe and put it on, then leaned down to kiss her cheek as she swished the mouthwash around. "I'm going to get dressed. See you downstairs before I leave."

CHAPTER 11

When the phone rang at 7:35 in the morning, Kathy knew it wouldn't be an enjoyable call. Nobody calls that early on a Friday morning unless it's for something that would require more work.

"Good morning, Kathy," Mary said on the other end.

Kathy closed her eyes and pinched the bridge of her nose, stifling a heavy sigh. She had worked so hard to have a nice, relaxing morning. She had gone for her run already, enjoying the crisp fall air and the smell of fallen leaves on the ground. So far her day had been peaceful…until she heard Mary's voice. "Good morning, Mary. How are you?"

"I'm stressed."

"Why's that?"

POLTERGEIST

She groaned dramatically. "Ugh! We have a problem."

"What's the problem?"

"The Lawrence Park Golf Club called me last night and they said they're short-staffed. They don't have any employees available to help us set up the tables for the shower! It's tomorrow! What are we supposed to do? We were counting on them to set those up and make sure there were eight to a table and that the tablecloths were laid out and the place settings were prepared. This is a disaster!"

"Okay, take a deep breath." Kathy kept her voice calm as she judged Mary for her perception of a "disaster." "What did you tell the club after they told you they couldn't help set up?"

"I said I'd have to get back to them with what I wanted to do. But I've been up all night and I just don't see how we can manage to get it all done tomorrow morning before the shower!"

"You know what? I'll call the club today on my lunch break and get it straightened out. There's an easy solution here, I know it." She rolled her eyes, grateful that this was a phone call and not another in person meeting.

"Did you ever call the caterers?"

"Between when I saw you last night and now? No, Mary, I need to wait for someone to be in the office." She bit her tongue after that. She hadn't intended to sound so snarky.

Mary huffed. "I see. Well. Don't you forget to call! And

after you've heard something, you give me a call right away! Promise? I need to know what's going on. I am the *grandmother*, you know."

"Yes, I will." Kathy forced kindness into her voice. She decided to leave out that she had a vested interest in this baby too. To put it Mary's way, she was the *aunt*, after all. "I gotta run, Mary. You have a good day. Don't worry about anything. I'll take care of it all."

"Call me when you do! And don't forget to call the caterers too!"

Kathy nodded, though she knew Mary couldn't see. "Yes. Both of them are on my list to call. Expect to hear back from me by one o'clock."

Hopefully putting a time on it would keep Mary at bay until then, she thought to herself. *Or maybe I just gave her a deadline that she's going to hold me to.*

"Have a good day," Kathy offered before she hung up.

Once she was off the phone, she took a deep breath to calm herself down. Mary had a way of getting under everyone's skin. Throughout the planning process of this baby shower, Kathy felt for Samantha back when she had planned her wedding. And a baby shower wasn't nearly the spectacle event that a wedding was.

Kathy stepped over to the counter and finished making her lunch. She had only started it when the phone rang.

"Morning," Steven said when he entered the kitchen in

his blue dress shirt and black slacks. He stepped around Kathy and grabbed a box of cereal from the cupboard.

She shook her head. "Your mother is a piece of work."

"Is she giving you a hard time planning the shower?"

"Not exactly. She's just…high maintenance."

He laughed. "Yeah, that sounds like her. But I appreciate you including her in the plans. It means a lot to her, even if she has a funny way of showing it."

"Yeah," Kathy said with a sigh. She knew it was the right thing to do too, but it was still difficult.

Samantha came down after a few more minutes. By then, Kathy had finished making her sandwich and was putting everything in a brown paper bag. Steven sat at the table eating his breakfast and reading the paper.

"And there she is!" Kathy said. "The star of the show herself!"

Samantha grumbled and crouched to the cabinet below, where she reached for a pot.

"What are you making?" Kathy asked.

"Pasta. It's what I'm in the mood for."

Kathy and Steven exchanged looks.

"For breakfast?" Kathy asked. "I think there's some leftover spaghetti in the fridge."

Samantha opened the fridge and looked at the selections. "I don't want the sauce, just the pasta with…hmm…oooh! Yes!" She reached for something and came out with a jar of pickles. "Pickle juice over the pasta sounds delicious."

Kathy turned away. "All right then. I'm going to work before you gross me out by actually eating that."

CHAPTER 12

- OCTOBER 1934 -

Now that Henry's mother was gone, he always made sure to rush home after school. Not because he wanted to spend anymore time there. Actually, he'd rather stay in class and work on school work all night long if it meant not having to go back to that house. Without his mother, it no longer felt like a home. Not that it ever really did to begin with.

No, Henry had to rush back because he had chores to do. Everything his mother had done before she had passed, plus the chores Henry had been doing on his own. It was a lot for a ten-year-old to handle, but he managed most days.

Henry arrived home in a hurry and tossed his backpack on the couch. The strap caught a lamp on the end table, knocking it to the floor with a crash.

The boy froze as he stared at the mess. His father wouldn't be happy about that. But he'd also be home in twenty minutes and he'd expect dinner to be ready. Henry didn't have time to clean up the mess.

He made a decision and turned to the kitchen to prepare their meal. If he hurried with that, he might be able to get the glass cleaned up before his father came home. Maybe his father wouldn't even notice the lamp was missing.

It was a good plan, except that Henry was still learning how to cook. His mother had only been gone a week and a half, meaning that Henry had only been preparing meals for that long. After fifteen minutes, the meat had dried out from frying on the stove too long, the baked potatoes were still hard from not being in the oven long enough, and there was eggs and seasoning and flour all over the prep table and the floor.

As hard as he tried, the meal was a disaster. His father would *not* be happy.

Henry was stuck. If he started over, his father would know that he had wasted food. But if he didn't start over, his father would be irate that the food tasted so bad. And there was still the lamp.

The front door swung open suddenly and his father stepped in. Henry jumped, then froze. His heart raced wildly in his chest.

"What the hell happened here?" his father asked, indicating the lamp.

Henry stayed where he was and tried his best to salvage dinner. Maybe if he added more seasoning to the meat and put the potatoes back in the oven he could—

"And why the hell does it smell like something's burning in here?" His father stepped into the kitchen. "What are you doing? Burning the place down? I thought you could handle it. You expect me to pay for a cook just because you can't figure out how to make something edible?"

"S-sorry," Henry stammered. "I couldn't remember how long to cook everything for and I was trying to—"

"Enough with these excuses! I come home after a hard day's work and expect to not have to do anything around here. And you're creating a bigger mess!"

Henry bowed his head, ashamed that his father was right. He was failing. He didn't know how his mother had gotten it all done.

"You deserve a spanking," his father said.

Fear crippled Henry as he stared into his father's eyes. His father had threatened spankings before and only delivered on them a few times. Usually, his mother protected him from them. Henry's father had a habit of getting out of hand when he was trying to "discipline."

In an instant, Henry pulled himself out of his fear and made the decision to run. He dashed up toward his bedroom, thinking that his father would let him stay in there, as he always had. If he didn't emerge until later, maybe his father would forget the whole thing. Henry could sneak down after his father had fallen asleep and find something to fill his belly.

Except Henry's father followed him up the stairs this time, crashing through Henry's bedroom door and knocking him to the hardwood floor.

He vaulted on top of the boy, pinning him beneath him. "Don't you *ever* run away from me again, boy!"

Henry recoiled from his father's face, which was only inches from his own. This wasn't something he had ever done before, but it wasn't surprising. Before Henry's mother passed, punishments would often start to escalate toward moments like this. It was always Henry's mother who had stepped in between them. Who took the brunt of his father's anger.

Now he had no one.

The first punch was right in Henry's gut, leaving him breathless and queasy. For several minutes, he thought he was going to throw up right there on his bedroom floor. But the feeling passed.

"You disrespect me again, boy, and I'm not going to stop at one."

Henry froze, nervously eyeing his father.

His father shook the boy. "You hear me!?"

Nodding, Henry sputtered out a "Yes."

His father stood, still seething with anger. Henry didn't dare move. Finally, his father spit on him just before storming out of the room.

POLTERGEIST

"Clean up downstairs and make me something I can actually *eat* for dinner," he said. "I'm going outside to do work, because apparently that's all I'm good for."

CHAPTER 13

Kathy hated using her lunch break for errands, but the phone calls needed to be made. Usually, she spent her break quietly in staff room with a good book as she ate her lunch. It wasn't until she started working for Dr. Newberg that she really got into reading for fun. After taking a couple English classes in college where reading difficult texts was a homework assignment, she thought she'd be turned off to all books. She was happy to find out that that wasn't the case.

Which was why spending her half hour of freedom in the middle of the day making phone calls was so frustrating for her. She had already called the caterers and the golf club and straightened everything out with both of them. Now the line was ringing as she made the dreaded call to Mary to update her on what she had come up with.

"Hello?"

"Hi Mary, it's Kathy."

"Oh hello, dear! Did you call the caterers and the club?"

"Yup." Kathy nodded, smiling to help bring cheer to her voice. Otherwise, she probably wouldn't have much patience with Mary. It was the same tactic she used at work with difficult patients or insurance companies over the phone.

"So the caterers are okay with the schedule change?"

"They said it'd actually be easier for them," she said. "That way they don't have to clear room halfway through the shower. Or fuss with putting out the desserts and having people take from the table before it's ready. It'll be less of a distraction for everyone."

"Oh good. Yes, I did think it would be distracting if they put out the desserts later."

Kathy rolled her eyes. Mary *always* had to know the right answer, even if it meant changing her story.

"And the club?" Mary asked. "What did they say?"

"Well…they're short-staffed, as they told you."

Mary groaned.

"*But* we worked out a plan," Kathy added quickly. "They don't have any events tonight, so I said that we could set up the tables and everything ourselves. We'll just have to take everything down tomorrow after the shower, but maybe we can recruit some of the guys to help us."

"I can't tonight!" Mary nearly shouted. "I have a hair appointment! I wanted to get it done before the shower tomorrow." She groaned again.

"It's okay," Kathy said. "Just take a breath. I'll be there and so will Steven and Samantha—"

"Samantha can't lift anything!"

"But she can help lay out the tablecloths. And if she needs to take a break, then she takes a break. It's not a big deal. We could use Marty's help, though, if you want to send him. Is he free?"

"Uh…I believe so, yes—so you're saying you don't need me?"

More like we don't want you to drag it out, Kathy thought. "If you want to swing by after you're done with your hair appointment, you can help with the finishing touches."

That offer seemed to make Mary breathe easier. "Oh. Okay. I think that'll work."

"Okay? So problem solved?"

"Yes, well, I feel better knowing it's all taken care of. I'll see you later, dear. Bye!"

Kathy hung up the phone and rolled her eyes. Of course Mary didn't offer a "thank you" at all.

Checking the time, she saw that there were only a few minutes left of her break. She sighed, glancing at the book she had brought with her. She had borrowed it from the library and it was due back by Monday, but there was no way she was going to get to reading it today.

Poltergeist

Back out at her post at the front desk, Kathy took the "out for lunch" sign down and slid open the glass divider between the office area and the waiting room. The next appointment was in ten minutes, so the patient would be arriving soon.

Kathy looked down at her list of things to do that she had written before lunch. As she refreshed her mind, she heard the wind rush in as the door opened from outside.

There's that patient now, she thought.

When she looked up, though, she saw a friendly, familiar face smiling at her.

"Jeff! What are you doing here?"

From behind his back, he pulled out a bouquet of flowers. "Just wanted to bring you something nice at work."

She took them and sniffed the blooms, smiling at the gesture. "They're beautiful. Thank you. But…how did you know where I worked?"

"You mentioned it last night on our date. I wasn't sure exactly *where* Dr. Newburg's office was, so I checked the phone book."

"You checked the entire phone book just to bring me flowers?"

"Just to see you smile."

"Well, that was very sweet. Thank you." She looked around, trying to find something to use as a vase until she could get home and put them on display properly. She found a coffee mug left by one of the nurses and figured she could clean it out and make due until she got home.

"I had a lot of fun last night," he said. "I would love to go out again sometime. Are you free tonight?"

She made a face. "Actually, I'm not. My sister's baby shower is tomorrow and I'm kind of putting it on. Tonight we're setting everything up." A thought occurred to her. "Hey, are you free? Do you want to swing by to help lug tables? It's okay if you don't want to, but we could use some extra manpower."

Kathy hoped she wasn't going to regret this decision. She had only been on one date with Jeff. She wasn't even sure if she saw a future with him yet. Was she prepared for Samantha's questioning of him? She usually liked to date guys for a bit before she put them through her sister's "screening" process.

"Yeah, I'll be there. What time? And where?"

"I haven't thought of the time yet. Maybe…six o'clock? It's at the Lawrence Park Golf Club. Do you know where that is?"

"Oh sure. I play golf there with my dad sometimes over the summer."

"Perfect! So I'll see you later?"

"Definitely."

"And maybe tomorrow night for that date?"

He gave her a lopsided grin. "Can't wait."

CHAPTER 14

Steven loved the lunch dates with his wife. Whenever they got the chance to be alone together, he jumped at the opportunity. He admired and respected Samantha's relationship with her sister, but it often interfered with the romance in their marriage. So taking her to lunch in the middle of a workday was the perfect time to sneak in some extra moments with her.

They often ate at a little café downtown. It wasn't fancy, but it had room enough where they could sit and have a bit of privacy. Samantha often arrived first because her office was closer and today was no exception. When Steven walked in, she was looking up at the menu chalkboard above the serving line, trying to decide on her order. There were cobwebs and ghosts drawn on the board for Halloween, as well as a sign advertising the café's latest orange-tinted drink.

"Know what you're getting?"

Samantha jumped when he spoke into her ear.

Steven smiled as his wife swatted at him.

"That was rude," she said. "No. I haven't decided yet. I just got here."

"Busy morning?"

"Mr. Marsden dumped all the quarterly reports on my desk because I'm *such a good worker*." Her voice grew nasally as she intimidated him. "I swear, sometimes I think if I just did mediocre work then I wouldn't have so much of it to do."

"I'm sorry. Do you even have time to take a lunch?"

"Time or not, I'm taking it," she said. "Besides, I walked here and my feet are killing me, even with just the two blocks."

"Take a seat and I'll order for both of us."

"Thanks." She told him what she wanted and then ventured off to a booth by the window.

When Steven brought their food over—sandwiches and two small bags of chips—Samantha had stretched out on her side of the booth with her feet up on the seat.

"They're all swollen." She stretched across the booth to rub her feet.

"You shouldn't have walked here then," he said. "Do you want me to help you walk back?"

"No, I don't want you to help me." She rolled her eyes. "How humiliating would that be, to have my husband escort me back to the office?"

Steven decided to let it go. Any other time, Samantha might like that idea, thinking it cute or romantic. Today, she was clearly in a bad mood.

He passed her the sandwich he'd ordered for her and a bag of chips. "Are you sure you wanted a tuna salad with mustard and ketchup on it?"

She wrinkled her nose. "I know. I'll probably end up scraping most of the tuna off."

He looked at her, trying to determine if she was serious. Her pregnancy cravings had always been a little strange, but if he understood her correctly, all she really wanted was two pieces of bread with ketchup and mustard on them. It sounded terrible to him, but he had learned over the course of her pregnancy not to question it.

As Samantha doctored her sandwich, she said, "I think now's a good time to talk about the house we saw yesterday."

"Yeah. I was thinking about it and I like the location. It would certainly be closer for both of us to get to work, but I just don't think it's going to work out overall."

"Exactly." She licked her thumb clean of the tuna salad she had scraped onto the wrapper. "It's way over our heads. There's too much to do to it."

Steven nodded and took a bite of his own sandwich.

"Maybe we can have Rupert find something that doesn't need as much work."

"Honestly, Steven, you need to give up on this whole fixer-upper idea," she said. "You're not handy and, working as an accountant in an office all day, you'll probably never be. We need something that's more move-in ready where we can hire someone to do little fixes here and there."

Steven was struck by her words. Her bluntness. How casually she had insulted him. That wasn't like Samantha.

Then again, Samantha hadn't been *Samantha* lately. He wanted to use her pregnancy to explain it away, but the mood swing had come on so suddenly that he wasn't sure. Maybe there was something more going on here, but he couldn't figure out exactly what.

He would have to ask Kathy later. As much as he hated to admit it, nobody knew Samantha better than her sister.

"So," he said, sidestepping her insult, "do you want to look for a house that's been recently flipped?"

She finished chewing a hefty bite of her sandwich. She'd already worked her way through half of it. Apparently the inner contents of the sandwich would've only slowed her down. "Honestly, with the baby coming in a couple months, it's really stupid to be looking for a house at all. I mean, even if we found one today that we loved, by the time we put an offer on it and bought it and moved in, we'd have a newborn on our hands. I wouldn't be able to help much, if any at all. You can only do so much because you're not exactly Mr. Muscles."

Again, Steven felt the sting of her attack. What she said was true, but she'd never been so mean about it.

"We'd have to hire movers and that'd be a lot of coming and going with a newborn," Samantha went on, oblivious to his reaction. "Not to mention the *cost*. Where would we be getting this money from? Neither of us are millionaires. We'd be shelling out all of this money for a house we'd have to carry a mortgage on. It just financially doesn't make sense, either. I mean, we're both accountants. Lets be responsible with our money."

She took another bite, ketchup and mustard pooling in the corners of her mouth. She wiped it away and swallowed. "I think you're just going to have to suck it up and get used to the fact that we live with Kathy. At least until we have a good handle on the baby. Maybe when they turn a year old we can revisit this idea about getting our own place."

Steven stared at his wife, now completely convinced that she wasn't acting like herself. That something else was going on.

"Okay," he said. "So we'll wait."

With her sandwich now gone, Samantha reached for the bag of chips and popped it open. "Yeah. Living with Kathy won't be too terrible. I mean, she can be annoying sometimes, but I guess I've gotten used to it being her sister and all. And it's not like *she's* going anywhere. If anything, maybe we can make the best of the situation and have her help us raise this kid. That'll actually give her some purpose in life now that she's a college dropout."

Silently, Steven continued eating his lunch. As harsh as it was to admit, he was glad to know that Samantha's jabs had also been extended to her sister and weren't solely directed at him.

But that only confirmed that something was going on with his wife.

CHAPTER 15

After work later that day, Kathy rushed home as fast as she could. That meant power-walking in the on-and-off October drizzle. She had been starting to take the bus now that the weather was turning colder, but it wasn't always reliable and sometimes it took her up to thirty minutes to go down the street. Walking was usually faster.

With a stroke of pure luck, Kathy reached the front door of their Victorian house just as Samantha pulled in the driveway, followed a minute later by Steven.

Kathy unlocked the door and escaped the damp, wet weather.

By time Samantha and Steven got inside, Kathy had already fixed her hair in the foyer mirror and was surveying the rest of the damage the rain had done to her looks.

"You walked?" Samantha hung up her purse on a hook near the entry.

"I had to get home quick," Kathy said. "Actually, the three of us need to turn around and head right to the golf club to set up for tomorrow's shower."

"Right *now*?" Samantha asked.

"I thought they were going to take care of that?" Steven asked.

"They're short-staffed," Kathy explained. "But we need to go now because there's only going to be someone there until about seven, which gives us—" She checked her watch. "—only about an hour and a half to get there and set up."

Samantha let out an exaggerated sigh. "Great. Just what I want to do on my Friday night."

"Sorry," Kathy said. "It shouldn't take us long. It's just that this is the best time to set up rather than trying to rush around tomorrow morning—where are you going? We have to leave right now."

Samantha began to walk off to the kitchen. "Give me a second! I'm hungry!"

Kathy and Steven followed her into the kitchen.

"Sam, we can get pizza or something on the way home," Kathy said.

"I don't want pizza." She reached for a banana, then opened the cupboard for the jar of peanut butter.

"If you wanted to stay home, that would be fine," Steven suggested. "As pregnant as you are, you shouldn't be lifting much anyway."

Samantha hooked an eyebrow. "So you're saying I'm worthless?"

"No, that's not—"

"I'll have you know that I'm *creating life* here," she pushed. "And let me remind you that *you* did this to me."

"Okay! Okay!" Kathy called out before she entered any awkward conversations about their sex life. "Sam, are you coming or not?"

"I'm coming." Samantha fished for something in the silverware drawer.

"Then hurry up and make your sandwich and let's go."

"Oh, I'm not making a sandwich." She produced a spoon, then grabbed the jar of peanut butter and tucked it under her arm. Making sure to grab her banana on the way, she started toward the front door.

Kathy and Steven exchanged looks, then Kathy shrugged and started to follow her sister, but Steven caught her arm.

"Hey, real quick before we go," he whispered when Samantha was out of earshot. "I want you to keep an eye on Samantha."

"Why? What's going on?"

"I'm worried about her," he said. "I think maybe something…*magical* might've happened to her."

"Magical how?"

He shook his head. "I don't know, exactly. But she's been very snappish and rude all day. It's not like her."

"Well, she's seven months pregnant…" Kathy started to the door, but Steven reached for her again.

"And she just started being this rude all of a sudden."

Kathy stared up at him as she recalled her sister's actions over the last couple days. It was true. Samantha seemed grumpier than her normal self. Even grumpier than her pregnant self. "Are we sure it's not just hormones?"

Steven shrugged. "I suppose it could be. But I just figured with everything else that you guys encounter, we might want to consider the possibility that there's more to it than hormones."

"Hel-lo!" Samantha called as she stepped into the doorway of the kitchen. She had a spoonful of peanut butter hanging out of her mouth. Around the spoon, she asked, "Are we going or not?"

"Be right there," Kathy said. "Why don't you go start the car? Keep it warm."

Samantha rolled her eyes and then headed for the front door.

It wasn't until Kathy heard it shut that she told Steven, "I don't know of anything that could've happened in the last couple days. Everything's been pretty quiet."

"I know," he admitted. "I just thought—"

"It's better to be safe than sorry." She nodded. "You're right. I'll keep my eye out for any other strange behavior."

CHAPTER 16

Kathy waved to Marty Harper as he pulled into the parking lot. Kathy, Samantha, and Steven were just walking into the club and decided to wait in the lobby until Marty caught up.

The rain had picked up, so Steven stood at the door to hold it open for his father, who came trotting up with a wide-brimmed hat that he held on top of his head with his hand.

"It's really opening up out there," he said with a laugh. "How you folks doing? It's good to see you again."

Steven hugged his father. "Are you ready to set up tables?"

"That's what I've been told," he said. "Your mother will be stopping by later after her hair appointment. Samantha, you look fantastic. How are you feeling?"

"Like a whale," she said as she hugged him too.

"Sam, you've got some schmutz on your mouth." Kathy licked her thumb and reached for the corner of her sister's mouth, where remnants of the peanut butter remained.

"Sorry," Samantha murmured after she had been cleaned up. "I had a little snack on the way here."

Kathy and Steven exchanged looks. It had been more than a snack, with Samantha finishing nearly half the jar of peanut butter and the banana she had brought.

"You're not going to help move tables, are you?" Marty asked. "You should sit this one out. You don't want to do anything that could hurt the baby."

Samantha's jaw tightened. "You don't think I know my own limit? Do you think I'm too stupid to realize when I'm getting too tired or putting too much strain on my body? Or do you just think I'm going to be a horrible mother?"

"Sam," Kathy said as a warning.

"No, I'm tired of people pointing out all of my limitations," she persisted.

"I didn't mean to—"

"You didn't *think*," she said. "All you see is a fragile, fat woman whose only purpose in life is to care for her child. Well, guess what? I'm still my own person, even though I'm also a mother now."

"Sam!" Kathy said more forcefully.

"Come on, Dad." Steven put his arm around Marty's

shoulders and led him into the clubhouse. "Sam's been feeling a little self-conscious lately…"

"That was rude," Kathy told her sister once they were alone.

The older witch shrugged. "He pissed me off."

"I thought you liked Marty?" He was usually the favorite of her in-laws because he was always so happy and go-with-the-flow. Unlike his wife.

"I do, but am I supposed to smile and take it when someone treats me like an invalid? I mean, I'm pregnant, not crippled. And even if I were crippled, I could still contribute something."

Kathy couldn't argue with that. "Just try to be nicer. We're all here for you, remember."

"Correction: you're all here for the *baby*."

"Which, as you've pointed out numerous times, is still growing inside you," Kathy said. "So until he or she comes out, all the baby stuff is for you too."

"Whatever," Samantha said. "Can we get this over with so I can go home?"

Kathy put up her hands in a surrender gesture and her sister walked into the clubhouse. Meanwhile, Kathy looked on and wondered the same thing Steven had been wondering: what the hell was going on with Samantha?

CHAPTER 17

- OCTOBER 1934 -

Henry didn't dare move. He barely allowed himself to *breathe*. He stood in his closet in the dark, listening as his father called for him from downstairs.

"I know you're home, boy! Where the hell are you?"

All Henry wanted was a break. One day off from having to do everything around the house. And he thought he was going to get it when his father said he was working late tonight. Apparently those plans had changed and when Henry heard his father come through the front door, he had dropped the book he was reading and ran into the closet to hide.

Except, the front door being unlocked and the lights on downstairs told his father that he was home.

"I'm not about to play hide-and-seek," his father called. "What the hell have you been doing? This place looks like a mess!"

Henry began shaking. So bad that he needed to let go of the door handle or risk giving away his position.

Not only had he had to take on all of his mother's chores since she had passed, but he had also inherited the abuse. The beatings for not having dinner ready on time. The taunts and teases for doing "woman's work," even though it was expected of him. The fear of doing something wrong that would result in a slap or a punch or a kick from his father.

All of it only added to the rage building inside Henry.

"You're making me mad, boy," his father said. "There are certain expectations when you come home. Rules you need to follow. If you don't do your chores, then there's going to be punishment. You can't—"

The abrupt end to his mantra put Henry on high alert. Was his father on his way up to his room? Did he go outside? Did he find some other evidence that Henry was hiding from him?

The silence was terrifying.

"Oh hello," his father said in a voice that wasn't really his own. It was kind, sweet, much like the one he had used at Henry's mother's funeral. "You know, I don't know where Henry ran off to, but I don't think he'll be gone too much longer."

Poltergeist

There was someone at the door.

Henry bolted from his hiding place and raced down the stairs. If there was a neighbor at the door, his father wouldn't hit him. Not in front of someone. Maybe Henry could sneak out of the house. Come up with an excuse to have dinner at someone else's house. Breathe easy for one night, even if that meant a bigger punishment when he finally came back to this place he was supposed to call home.

As Henry barreled down the stairs, he saw Mrs. Johnson from across the street standing in the doorway. His father's arm leaned up against the doorframe in an effort to keep her from coming in any further.

"There he is!" she said brightly.

Henry's father turned and sneered at him. "Yes, there he is."

"I just wanted to check on you two," she said. "See if everything is okay."

"Why wouldn't they be?" His father turned back to her, his coolness wearing off with his growing anger.

"Well, with Helen gone, I just thought..." She strengthened her resolve and said, "To be quite honest, Ivan, I'm here because I've been hearing a lot of...*noise* coming from this house. It's been going on for a while now and I've always been meaning to say something but with Helen gone—well, I just want to make sure the boy is taken care of."

"The boy is fine."

Henry stepped closer, tried to get around his father to escape outside. Maybe Mrs. Johnson could help him if he could manage to get out of the clutches of his father.

Too late. As Henry got under his father's arm, he hooked it around the boy's neck possessively. Henry winced in pain.

"Henry and I are doing just fine."

Mrs. Johnson studied Henry's expression, then turned back to Ivan. "Well, I just wanted to—"

"The boy has been acting up lately," he said. "That's why you've been hearing yelling." He nudged his son. "Go on and apologize for bothering this poor woman."

"Nonsense, you don't have to—"

Henry's father smacked him in the back of the head. "*Apologize!*"

Gulping, the boy said, "I'm sorry Mrs. Johnson."

Her mouth hung open as she studied the two of them. Then she looked back up to his father and offered a pleasant smile that didn't quite reach her eyes. "Perhaps he's having a hard time dealing with his mother's passing. Maybe he needs a female figure in his life. I would be happy to have him over for dinner a few times a week if that would—"

"I'm not going to reward his bad behavior with visits to the neighbors," his father said abruptly. "I need to be able to discipline my son in my own way."

"Right, but if—"

"Is there anything else you *need*, Mrs. Johnson?"

Her eyes lingered on Henry, who tried to plead with her wordlessly. "No. I was just checking up."

"Well then, I better get back to getting this one back on track." Without another word, he shut the door right in Mrs. Johnson's face.

Henry's head was still locked under his father's arm. After the door was shut, he pushed away and was finally able to free himself.

"Did you say something to her?" his father asked.

Henry shook his head rapidly.

"So now we have strangers coming and knocking on our door to check on us? Do you know how embarrassing that is?"

Henry didn't say anything.

His father grabbed a fistful of his hair and yanked back his head until their eyes met. "You've been telling everyone I'm a bad father, haven't you?"

"N-no!" Henry stuttered. "I haven't said anything!"

It didn't matter. His father was already mad.

Using all of his strength, he tossed Henry to the floor.

The boy reached up and massaged his scalp, grateful to be away from his father's grip, even if the fall did hurt.

"I think you deserve a spanking," he said. "First you hid from me, then you got the neighborhood riled up against me. What's next, boy? You going to kill me in my sleep?" He charged at his son, but Henry took off toward the kitchen.

He tried to make it to the back door, but it was still locked.

He managed to get one of the locks opened, but by then his father had his hands on the back of his shirt.

"Don't you run away from me, boy! You look at me while I'm talking to you!"

Unable to free himself, Henry instead looked around for a weapon. Something that would get his father to lose his grip enough so that Henry could escape outside.

His hand grabbed ahold of the handle on the frying pan, still on the stove from that morning's breakfast. Swinging it up, the pan collided with his father's face, causing a satisfying *crunch*.

Instantly, Henry was released. He turned and saw all of the blood spilling onto the floor and froze.

What if he seriously hurt his father? What if they needed to go to the hospital? How would they explain it?

The pause was a costly one and his father let out a roar and grabbed Henry by the front of his shirt.

"Sorry!" the boy blurted, but it was too late. The damage had been done.

Flinging open the basement door, his father tossed Henry down the stairs. He tumbled, smacking his head against a wooden step, releasing the pan as he fell so that it clambered down the stairs until it came to rest on the dirt floor at the bottom. Henry, however, managed to grab the handrail. He twisted his wrist, but he managed to stop himself halfway down the stairs.

Poltergeist

"Maybe some time down here will help you think about what you've done!"

The basement door slammed shut and a lock slid into place.

CHAPTER 18

Steven helped his father unfold a circular table in the corner. It was the last one they needed to bring out from storage. All that was left was to pull out the chairs and lay the tablecloths.

"Do you think this is good?" Steven asked.

Marty stood back with his hands on his hips and looked at the arrangement. With a grin he said, "You realize your mother's going to have something to say regardless of how we set everything up?"

"Isn't that why you married her?" Steven asked with his own smirk. "For her opinions?"

Marty smiled. "All I'm going to say is: sure."

Steven laughed, then stopped when he saw Samantha

carrying two chairs out from the storage room. "Sam! What are you doing?" He rushed over to take the chairs from her. "You're not supposed to be doing this kind of stuff!"

She glared at him and he knew she was probably embarrassed for having been yelled at in front of Kathy and Marty. "Then what the hell am I supposed to do?"

"Why don't you help your sister with the tablecloths?" he suggested. "My dad and I can get the chairs. It'll be easier for you to do the tablecloths without the chairs anyway."

"Are you even *ready* for us to do that? As far as I can tell, you guys are taking your sweet ol' time with the tables. *Some* of us would like to go home!"

Steven forced himself to stay calm, but it was hard when his wife was clearly on the offensive. "Yes, we're ready."

She started to walk off to the storage room, where Kathy hung out in the doorway, waiting to help.

Steven grabbed his wife's arm to stop her from walking away from him. He didn't say anything until she met his eyes. "I just want you to be careful. You're not supposed to be pushing it in your third trimester."

"I was carrying chairs, Steven. Not lifting weights."

"You may as well have been," he said. "You're actually lucky you don't have worse pregnancy side effects than you do."

"Oh, so I should be grateful that everyone is treating me like I'm helpless?"

As much as he tried, he couldn't keep the edge from his

voice. "Of course not, but I don't want you to hurt yourself—or the baby—doing something you could've avoided."

"You need to back off."

"You're being reckless!" he snapped. "You're *always* reckless. But this time, it's not just you that you're hurting, it's the baby. *Our* baby. It may be inside you, but it's mine just as much as it's yours!"

"Oh, I think I see your mother pulling in!" Marty called out suddenly.

Steven looked around and realized that he and Samantha had been arguing in the center of the room, causing a scene. Luckily, it was just his father and Kathy, but it was still embarrassing.

He released his wife's arm and took in deep breaths to calm himself down.

"I'm going to go down and greet her with an umbrella," Marty said. "We'll be back soon."

It was a warning that whatever *discussion* the couple was having should be over by the time Steven's mother came upstairs.

When his father was gone, Steven sighed and started, "Look, I'm so—"

"Is this how you're going to talk to our kid?" Samantha asked. "Lash out at them in front of everyone and scar them for life? It's a good thing we have good insurance, because they're going to be in therapy for their whole life."

"Hey!" Steven roared. "Don't you *dare* even think that!"

Samantha shrugged.

"You really think I'm going to mess up our kids by yelling at them?" he asked. "What about all the witchy things *you're* going to bring home to them?"

"At least I'll be able to protect them."

"Will you? Or will you be inviting the thing that's going to *kill* them into our lives?"

Two things happened in that instant. The speaker system around the room squealed with irritating feedback, even though nobody was anywhere near the microphone or any of the sound equipment.

At the same moment, Samantha's eyes flared and she threw out her arms toward her husband. Next thing Steven knew, he was flying backward and crashing hard into one of the tables he and Marty had set up. It collapsed under his weight and Steven felt the sharp pain in his back as he made impact.

He struggled to get up, but the wind had been knocked out of him. Worse, the fight had been knocked out of him as well. Did his wife just really attack him? More than that, did she really think those things she said about him? About how he would be as a father?

That hurt worse than the pain he currently felt in his back.

CHAPTER 19

"Sam!" Kathy called out as she ran to Steven's aid. He lay flat on his back, groaning in pain. "Are you okay? Are you hurt?"

He took a deep breath that she could tell brought a flash of pain, but he shook his head. "I'm okay. Or I will be. Just add another bruise to the collection."

Kathy narrowed her eyes at the comment, but turned to her sister instead. "What the hell was that?"

Samantha shrugged. "He was getting on my nerves."

"What is *wrong* with you? Do you even realize what you just did?"

The older sister rolled her eyes. "Look, I don't need a lecture from you too. Okay? I'm tired and I'm bored and *apparently* I can't do anything to help."

Kathy shook her head, still amazed by what she had just witnessed. Never in a million years did she think that Samantha would attack Steven like that. And what kind of power was that? Samantha's specialty was the mind, not telekinetics.

"I don't even know why I came," Samantha went on. "So if you don't want me to actually do anything, then I guess I'm done trying to help."

Without another word, she turned and disappeared into the next room, which overlooked the golf course.

Kathy turned back to Steven, who had managed to sit up. "Are you sure you're okay?"

He nodded. "I'll be fine. Just, help me up before my parents get in here. I don't want them to know what happened."

She took his hands and hauled him to his feet.

He cringed as he straightened out his back and reached around to rub it.

"Well," she said with a sigh, "I think it's safe to say that there's definitely something going on with Samantha."

"Something magical?"

"I think that's obvious. The way she threw you across the room was not something that she could normally do on her own."

"Any idea what it could be?"

"No," the witch admitted. "But we're going to figure it out."

"Do you think the speaker shrieks have anything to do with it?"

Kathy considered, but couldn't think of anything. She was about to say as much when Steven's parents walked through the doors into the clubhouse, cutting off any talk of the supernatural.

"Hello, my sweet boy—oh!" Mary stopped short when she saw the table.

"What happened?" Marty asked.

"It, uh…well…" Kathy stammered.

"I thought I could jump over it," Steven said. "I needed to let out some energy. I was wrong."

Mary rushed to his side. "You look like you're in pain, honey. Oh, come here and sit. We can take care of the rest." She tried to lead him over to one of the chairs that had pulled off the stack, but he shrugged away her help.

"It's okay, Mom," Steven said. "Really. I think I just need to loosen up the muscles." He pointed to the table. "Dad, do you want to help me fix this? Hopefully it's not broken."

"Where's Samantha?" Mary asked. "I thought she'd be here?"

"She is," Kathy said. "She just needed a break. Why don't you and I get started on the tablecloths?"

"Sure, dear, but first we need to fix these tables," Mary said. "Who set them up like this and what were they thinking? It'll never work like this!"

CHAPTER 20

Kathy carefully stepped down the stairs later that evening in her pajamas, making sure to avoid the areas of the steps that usually creaked. In her hands, she held *The Art of Magic*, which was the family magic book. She carried it into the living room, where Steven stood at the mirror in the corner with his T-shirt lifted, looking at his back. Kathy only glanced at first, but then she turned and stared.

Steven's back was covered in dark bruises.

"Oh my gosh," she murmured. "Is that just from the table?"

"No." He pointed to a red mark near his side. "Only this is from the table. Everything else just kind of appeared out of nowhere."

"You didn't get hit with anything?" Her gaze shifted from

looking at the reflection in the mirror to looking at his back directly.

"Not that I can remember. I just woke up today with all these bruises. Actually, I think there's more now than I saw this morning."

"Is this what you meant when you made that comment about adding another bruise to the collection?"

He nodded and lowered his shirt. "I don't know where they're coming from. Do you think it could be related to Samantha?" He reached for his bathrobe that he had laid over the back of the couch and put it on.

"I'm not sure how, but I guess anything is possible."

They quietly moved over to the couch, where Kathy lay the magic book on the coffee table and opened it. They needed to be quiet, since Samantha was fast asleep upstairs.

Before they left the golf club, Kathy and Steven had agreed to meet after Samantha had gone to bed.

"How long do you think we have until Samantha notices you're gone?" Kathy asked.

"Hopefully a while," he said. "She woke up when I got out of bed, but I just told her I was going to sit down here for a while until my back straightened out."

"Hopefully that will be enough to keep her suspicions at bay," Kathy murmured.

"Lately, it's so hard to read her," he said. "It's like she's not really my wife."

"Trust me, we're going to figure that out." Kathy turned to the magic book and began flipping through pages. "Okay, so I'm not exactly sure what we're looking for in here—" She stopped when she saw a red drop land on one of the pages. Looking up, she noticed Steven's nose dripping. "You're bleeding!"

"Shoot," he muttered as he cupped one hand under his nose and reached for a tissue with the other. He wiped away the blood and grabbed another tissue to try to clot the wound. "I've never really gotten nosebleeds before, but this is the second or third I've had in the last couple days."

"Hmm," Kathy mused.

Steven tilted his head back. "Do you think it's related?"

"Could be. It's like a phantom or something is beating you up."

"How does that explain what's going on with Samantha?" He pulled the tissue out and reached for another, dabbing at his nose to be sure the bleeding had stopped.

"I don't know," Kathy said. "Do you want me to help you get that cleaned up?"

"I'll get it later," he said. "I'm not sure if there's more coming. I just want to figure out what's going on with Samantha. Do you think it could just be her pregnancy?"

"Being pregnant won't magically make her a bitch," she said bluntly. "Being moody is one thing, but so far Samantha has been pretty even-tempered her whole pregnancy. This is more than that. Besides, she never used to have the power to throw people across the room. Apparently now she does."

"Are her powers just growing?"

Kathy shook her head. "I really don't think so. Her specialty is of the mind. And, okay, telekinesis is *technically* moving things with your mind, but what she did to you was advanced, magically speaking."

He raised his eyebrows and winced as he moved in his seat. "She definitely knew what she was doing."

"Somehow. Even if her powers were going to grow in that way, it would come after she'd been practicing and perfecting her other powers. Like a natural progression. And being pregnant has made her powers a bit unreliable—even the ones she had long-ago mastered—so I don't think that that's what's going on here."

Steven indicated *The Art of Magic.* "Do you think the answer is in this book?"

"Well, I think before the magic book can really help us, we need a better idea of what *could* be going on with her," Kathy said. "Let's retrace her steps over the last couple days. Maybe something happened to her that we're not thinking of."

He thought. "Um…for the most part she's pretty much just been going to work and coming home. That's what she did Monday and Tuesday. She did stop at the drug store after work on Wednesday to pick up some of her prenatal vitamins, but then she came right home. And then yesterday I picked her up from work so we could go look at a house near Gridley Park, but

I was with her the whole time. And she seemed fine yesterday."

"We can't overlook anything, though," Kathy said. "Or explain away any odd behavior. Visiting that house was something that was out of the ordinary for her, so we have to consider that something might've happened there. You said you were you with her the whole time?"

"Yes." Steven pulled out the last of the tissues that had been blotting his nose and added them to the bloodied pile sitting on the coffee table. "Well…no, I guess not."

"What do you mean?"

"I went down to check out the basement with the realtor. She stayed upstairs because she didn't want to breathe in anything toxic down there."

"How long were you away from her?"

"Maybe five minutes total. Nothing could've happened in that short of time, could it?"

Kathy shrugged. "It doesn't take long for some magic. Do you know if anything happened while you were down in the basement?"

"Not that I know of. Afterwards, she did say that she got a bad feeling about the whole house, but specifically the basement."

Kathy sighed. "I guess that's something, but it's not much. Was there anything in the house to indicate that it was magical? Maybe another witch family lived there before and left something?"

"I didn't see anything like that," he said. "The place was pretty empty. Why? Do you think she might be possessed by a ghost or something?"

The witch didn't answer. Her mind was working on an idea. Old houses, like the one they lived in, were filled with residual energies that most people didn't even notice. If the house had been sitting undisturbed, then touring the whole thing and talking about changes they were going to make to the structure might've upset the balance that had developed over the years of abandonment. And, in turn, upset any spirits that were residing there.

"Kathy?" Steven asked, breaking into her thoughts. "Are we looking at a ghost here? I guess it would be fitting for Halloween next week, but I don't like the idea of my pregnant wife being possessed by one. Does this mean the baby could be possessed too?"

Kathy ignored his wonderings. "Samantha mentioned that the house had been abandoned?"

"Yeah, it was empty."

"For how long?"

"Looked like it had been a while."

"Did you find any personal items in the house?"

"Samantha found a picture of the family that had lived there a long time ago," Steven said. "But she left the picture there. We didn't take anything with us."

"Interesting." Kathy didn't really have any experience with

possessions. Admittedly, she had a hard time separating reality and Hollywood in her mind. But the basics were still the same: disturb a highly-spiritual area and you could stir up bad spirits that brought bad luck.

Like bruises and nosebleeds.

"When did you first notice the bruises?" she asked.

"This morning—although, I guess my back hurt a little last night. I suppose I could've had one overnight and not paid much attention to it."

"And the nosebleeds?"

"The first one was last night. But it's also been dry outside, so it could be—"

"Have you heard any scratching?"

Steven furrowed his brow, but answered her questions anyway. "Um…yeah. Last night."

"I did too. I couldn't find the source, though."

"Neither could I," he said. "But I was distracted by the TV. You didn't happen to leave it on last night, did you?"

She shook her head. "No, I went upstairs before you guys. It was on?"

He nodded. "Just the TV—no lights or anything. It was weird. I thought someone had broken in."

"That is weird," she murmured, then remembered something. "Actually, last night when I heard the scratching, my radio turned on all on its own."

"You think that's connected?"

She shrugged again. "Could be. Just think about what happened right before Samantha threw you across the room today. The speakers gave that terrible feedback. The electronics are picking up on something."

"So what does all of this mean?"

Kathy flipped through the pages of the magic book until she landed on the section on spirits. "You're right. I think Samantha might be possessed."

"By a ghost?"

"Possibly. Definitely something that is pissed off that you guys were there," she said. "Although usually spirits like to stay in familiar places, so I'm not sure why it latched on to Samantha."

"So what do we do to get her…*un*-possessed?"

"Well, first we need to confirm that she actually *is* possessed," she said. "Right now all we have is speculation and I'd like something a little more concrete before we potentially scar my sister."

"How do we do that?"

"I need you to call that realtor first thing tomorrow and get us a showing in the morning."

"I don't know if he'll be able to—"

"We *have* to get this taken care of sooner than later," she said. "Preferably before the baby shower. Samantha's attitude is only growing worse and I don't want her to piss off everyone when they're only trying to do something nice for her. I know she would hate that too."

Steven nodded in agreement. "What are you going to do?"

"I'm going to have to call in a medium."

CHAPTER 21

- OCTOBER 1934 -

Henry sat at the top of the stairs, fussing with the back of the basement door. Even in the darkness, he noticed he could peel off the paint from the door. He had already worked off a lot, having a collection of paint peels in a pile. Using the frying pan that had fallen down the stairs with him, Henry had managed to put deep gouges in the door. He knew his father wouldn't be happy about that, but in the meantime, it gave Henry hope at an escape.

Besides, it was the only distraction he had from the painful hunger aching in his belly. He hadn't eaten since lunch at school the previous day. The only way he knew that time had passed was from the sun shining through the small sliver of a window down in the basement and the absence of his father's footsteps across the hardwood.

Henry wondered if his father even remembered that he was locked in the basement. But then, his father's nose was broken and probably throbbing with pain. It would serve as a constant reminder of what Henry had done.

And his father held grudges.

By Henry's estimation, it had been hours since his father had left for work. There was no telling when he would arrive home. Whether he would decide to work overtime or stop at the bar for a drink. Or, if he was feeling particularly cruel, he might just come home and let Henry sit in the basement as punishment for hurting him, all the while ignoring the boy's pleas to be freed..

The silence of the whole house also meant that there was no point in screaming. Based on Mrs. Johnson's visit the day before, the neighbors heard all of the noises coming from this house. None of them came to check on him—except Mrs. Johnson. And his father had told her exactly what he thought about that. Likely, she would never come back.

So yelling for help served no purpose. It seemed the whole neighborhood was frightened of his father and they weren't going to do anything to get on his bad side. Even if that meant that Henry had to suffer.

He was stuck.

After taking a short break from scraping the back of the basement door with the frying pan to give his arms a rest,

Henry jumped when the front door opened abruptly.

Through the crack under the basement door, Henry saw light emit from the other side as his father turned on a lamp in the kitchen.

Softly, Henry knocked on the door. "Father," he said. His voice was drier than he thought. It had been a while since he had had anything to drink. "I didn't mean to hurt you. I'm sorry for what I did. Can you please—"

The door suddenly shook violently near Henry's face and he jumped back, the frying pan colliding down the steps again. His father must've kicked the door.

"I better not hear you knocking on that door all night, boy!"

"But I'm hungry!"

"You're going to need to get used to that feeling if you don't shape up. Your mother adjusted just fine. You will too."

The mention of his mother got Henry's blood boiling. *Of course* his father put her through the same hell.

Balling his hands into fists, he beat them on the door as hard as he could. If his father didn't want to hear the knocking all night, that's exactly what Henry was going to do.

Henry was struck in the face as the door swung inward, hitting him right in the nose, hard enough that he thought it might be broken.

Guess he knew how his father felt.

Before Henry had a chance to assess any possible damage to his face, his father was inches away from him. He looked like hell. Two black eyes, dried blood crusted under his nose, and a violent look on his face.

His father reached out and grabbed Henry by his hair, forcing him to his feet.

"Ow!" Henry cried out, reaching up to try to pry his father's hand away.

"You should be *grateful* that sleeping in the basement is the only punishment I'm giving you after what you did." He pulled him close. "You see my face, boy? You see what you did? I've had people asking me all day what happened! Should I have told them that my son is a maniac? That he should be locked up?"

Henry just stared, wide-eyed and still trying to free himself from his father's grasp.

"Or maybe I should break your nose to make it even? What do you think? Is that fair? I think so."

The boy shook his head, cringing as the movement caused more pressure on his hair.

Suddenly, his father released him with a gentle push toward the stairs. Henry managed to grab on to the handrail so he didn't fall all the way down the stairs again, but he still lost his foot and stumbled back several steps. He looked up in time to see the door closing again. A second later, the lock slid into place, just like it had the day before.

Henry's father pounded his feet as he went up to the second floor, causing dust to fall down on top of Henry's head from the staircase above him.

Taking a seat on the small landing, Henry resumed scratching at the bottom of the door. His father didn't want him to knock, but at least this was something. Maybe, if Henry was lucky, he could scratch a hole right through the door and break out and never have to see his father again.

CHAPTER 22

What's the matter with you?" Kathy asked as she dipped her teabag in her cup the next morning. She stood at the kitchen island, a box of cereal beside her. She had already gone for her morning run and beaten everyone into the bathroom before it became Grand Central Station.

Steven had one hand on his back and groaned as he entered. "It was apparently a rough night." He labored to the chair by the island and sat. "Woke up with another nosebleed. Worse this time. All over the pillowcase. Samantha wasn't happy."

Kathy made a face. "I'm sorry."

"And more bruises," he added. "Not just on my back this time. I have one on my thigh, another on my stomach, and all the ones from my back feel like someone's been whacking me with a stick all night."

"You don't think it could be Samantha doing it, do you?"

He shook his head and winced, reaching up to rub his neck. "I don't think so. She was sound asleep. Last night I actually woke up from the pain and she was snoring away."

Kathy grinned. Her sister had started snoring since she'd become pregnant. It was a trait that the older witch was not too proud of. "So Samantha's awake then?"

Steven nodded. "She's in the shower."

"Then I'll have to make this quick. The baby shower is at twelve and it's…" She looked over at the clock. "…almost eight now. That only leaves us four hours to get everything fixed before the shower. Actually, less than that because I'll need to come back here at like eleven to get ready and it takes about twenty minutes to get to the golf club and we'll want to get there early…" She shook her head. "Anyway, my point is, we don't have much time."

"Right. So what's the plan?" He groaned again as he got up to fix himself a cup of coffee.

She watched him struggle for a second. "Are you even going to be able to do much?"

"I just need to stretch everything out." He reached for a bowl from the cupboard and took a deep breath to work through the ache. "I'll be fine."

"If you say so. Anyway, the plan for today is that I'm going to go to Mystic Treasures and see if Talia or Cassandra can get me any information about a medium who can meet us on short notice."

"You think we can get someone today?" He opened the box of cereal sitting beside Kathy and poured it into his bowl.

"I hope so," she said. "If not, I'll have to try to summon someone, but the last time I summoned someone I didn't get the results I wanted." She thought back to Samantha and Steven's wedding and the sloppy summoning spell she had performed.

"We don't want to add even more to our problems," Steven said.

"Right. While I'm doing that, I need you to call the realtor and see if he can get us a showing ASAP. If he agrees, meet me at Mystic Treasures so I can follow you to the house because I have no idea where it is." Kathy fixed her own bowl of cereal and carried it over to the table in the corner.

"On my list," he said. "Hopefully he can get us in this morning. I think he's retired and he just does this on the side now, but he might still have plans."

"Beg and plead with him then," Kathy said. "The sooner we can get this taken care of, the better."

"Get what taken care of?" Samantha asked as she stepped into the kitchen. Her wet hair was braided down her back—a method Kathy had showed her to get a nice wavy look.

"Just last minute details for the shower," Kathy lied. "Speaking of which, I need to head out this morning to run some errands."

Samantha grabbed the jug of orange juice from the fridge and a bowl from the cupboard and came over to sit with them. "How long do you think you'll be gone?"

"Most of the morning." Kathy noted the change back to normal for her sister. Cereal was certainly something she had enjoyed for breakfast before her pregnancy. Since then, Samantha had been having weird pregnancy cravings that resulted in odd breakfast choices. Pickles on toast. Spaghetti-O's and eggs. Leftover meatloaf and a slice of cake.

Samantha looked up at her husband. "Well, I guess it'll give us some time alone, honey."

Beneath the table, Kathy nudged him with her foot.

"I have some errands to run too," he said. "Kathy and my mom are using me as hired help."

"I see. So I'll be by myself."

"Think of it as a way to relax before everything starts to pick up." Kathy tried her best to sell it in a positive way.

The expectant mother reached for the orange juice and poured it into her cereal. "I suppose that's true. I can get some chores done around the house."

"Sam, did you mean to put OJ in your cereal?" Kathy asked.

She shrugged. "It sounded good."

"You really have a sweet tooth," Steven said.

"You try carrying around a watermelon in your belly and see if sugar helps comfort you through that exhaustion," she snapped. "Instead, you're leaving the fat lady home alone while the two of you run off together."

"No, we have separate errands," Kathy said, smiling at the truth in her statement.

Samantha took a spoonful of orange juice-soaked cereal in her mouth then waved her spoon at the two of them. "Seems awfully convenient that you two have errands to run at the same time together."

"It's Saturday morning. We're busy people." Kathy stood and carried her dishes to the sink. "Anyway, just keep an eye on the time. We have to be at the golf club at twelve. I'll try to be home by eleven to get ready and then we can head over. Oh, and I'm going to be taking your car this morning."

"Just remember to fill it up when you're done."

Kathy stepped out of the kitchen, grabbing the keys on the way. "Not a problem!"

CHAPTER 23

The bell rang above the door as Kathy stepped into Mystic Treasures. Talia stood behind the counter and smiled at her.

"Hi Kathy! How have you been?"

Kathy took a sweep of the store to make sure there weren't any other customers in there. It was a small occult shop, but it had its loyal followers, both magical practitioners and those who simply wished they were. It really depended on who was in the store that determined how openly they could discuss things magical.

"I've been okay," she said, stepping up to the counter. "But I need a little favor. You remember Steven, right? Samantha's husband?"

"How could I not? I'm the one who helped them become husband and wife."

Kathy smiled at the memory. Talia had been the one to officiate the wedding back in January. So much had changed since then, yet at the same time it was hard to believe that they had only been married for ten months.

"Anyway, he and I have been noticing that Samantha's been acting strange over the past couple days. There's more, that I won't get into, but we think that she may be possessed by a spirit of some sort."

"Oh my." Talia looked genuinely worried. "We mostly carry protection equipment, but we do have some herbs in stock that should also work at expelling negative energy. I don't know if that'll work on your spirit, but it's worth a shot."

"Well, I think I have another solution in mind. That is, if you could help point me in the right direction."

"How so?"

"Do you, by any chance, know of any mediums?"

Her face lit up. "Oh sure!" Beneath the counter, she reached for a notebook and flipped through the pages, running her finger down the list of handwritten entries. "Let's see here…we actually don't have too many mediums still practicing. Spirits mostly dwell in buildings and are usually stuck to that place. Nowadays, most people are tearing down old buildings and not trying to occupy them, which kills the spirit residing there in the process."

"If you know of anyone who might be available this morning, that would be ideal."

Talia shook her head as she scanned the list. "I'm not sure of their schedules, but I have their phone numbers here. You could call them. Ah! Here, we go. Good ol' Clarence."

"*Clarence?*"

The shopkeeper nodded. "Clarence Wellington. He's an older gentleman. A bit odd, but very good at what he does."

"I can handle odd. I'm just looking for answers." Kathy pointed to the phone sitting at the opposite end of the checkout counter. "Mind if I use that to make a call? I really don't want to wait until I get home. Not in front of my sister and all."

"Oh sure. Yeah, go ahead. Clarence is local."

Grabbing the notebook, Kathy held her finger to Clarence's entry, propped the phone between her cheek and her shoulder, and dialed in his number.

It rang once before a grouchy, phlegmy voice asked, "Who is this?"

She was taken aback for a moment, but quickly recovered. "Um, hi, Clarence? This is Kathy Walker. I got your information from Talia at Mystic Treasures?" She paused for recognition on his end, but he remained quiet. "Anyway, I have reason to believe my sister is possessed by a spirit of some sort and I would like your help in exorcising her."

Over her shoulder, she noticed Steven walking into the store. He looked around with cautious curiosity. She smiled, realizing that it was probably his first time in the store. It had a distinct incense smell to it and the inventory was especially out-of-the-ordinary.

"What kind of spirit are we talking about?" Clarence asked.

"I'm not exactly sure," she said. "My sister's husband has been waking up with bruises and nosebleeds, so I'm assuming not a nice one. Plus, my sister's attitude has been very bad lately. Not at all like she normally is."

"Evil spirits tend to just want you to stay out," he said. "I don't think you're looking at an evil spirit. Are you sure it isn't just your sister's time of the month?"

Kathy scoffed, shocked by the brazen assumption on Clarence's part. "She's pregnant, so definitely not. You know what? Can you hold on a second?"

His comment about Samantha had annoyed her, so she felt no remorse for putting him on hold. She held the phone against her chest and turned to Steven.

"Did you get ahold of the realtor?"

He nodded.

"And does he have an appointment available this morning?"

"He's actually on his way over to the house right now. Since it's an empty house he says he doesn't need to coordinate with the owners, which makes it easier."

"So I can invite the medium over to look at it with us?"

"I don't see why not."

Kathy went back to the phone call, where Clarence was

ranting on the other end.

"—will not be left on hold when *you* called *me*! If you want my help—"

"Clarence, sorry about that," she said, ignoring his irate tone.

"That was rude, young lady."

"Listen, we're actually heading to the house right now if you could take a look at it. See if there's any sign that the evil spirit had once been there and is now attached to my sister."

"We haven't discussed payment yet. Do you think you can afford me?"

She chuckled, only to defuse his ego. "Yes, I'm quite sure, Clarence. So will you meet us there?"

"What's the address?"

"Hang on." Again, she put the phone to her chest when she turned to Steven. "The address?"

"615 West 7th," he said.

She turned back to the phone, where Clarence was even angrier.

"—you put me on hold *one more time* and I don't care how much you'll pay me. I'll be done! You hear that? I'll be—"

"Yes, yes, I hear that," she said. "The address is 615 West 7th Street. Do you know where that is? It's near Gridley Park."

"I know exactly where that is! Lived in this damn city longer than you've probably been alive. What time are we talking?"

"Hmm…maybe fifteen minutes from now?"

"Are you *crazy*, lady?" he bellowed into the phone. "I can't do fifteen minutes! I could do an hour."

"Hang on a sec." She turned back to Steven. "He can't meet us, but he can meet us in an hour."

"Rupert's coming now," Steven said. "I don't want to hang out for an hour. Not if the time is really ticking to get this thing out of Samantha. Is there another medium you can contact?"

Kathy and Steven both turned to Talia, who was pretending not to listen in to the whole thing.

The shop owner shook her head. "Clarence is the best that I know of."

"Then Clarence is our guy." Kathy turned back to Steven. "So we look at the house alone and meet the medium later to go over all of our evidence in more detail. Does that work?"

He shrugged. "You tell me. I'm new to this."

She turned back to the phone. "Sorry again, Clarence."

"—absolutely a disgrace, this generation," he was saying to apparently no one in particular. "They only think about themselves and have no decency anymore—"

Kathy smiled, enjoying the fact that this rude old man did not take kindly to being treated the same way he had treated her. "We can meet you in an hour, but not at the house. Do you have somewhere else that we can meet?"

"Don't you dare put my on hold again!"

"I wouldn't dream of it, Clarence. Does an hour work for you?"

There was silence on the other end, then, "We can meet at my studio. It's at 326 East 21st Street. It's a three-story white house with a turret. You can't miss it."

"Sounds good, we'll see you—" She pulled the phone away from her ear and looked at it, not at all surprised that he had hung up on her.

"Are we good to go?" Steven asked.

She nodded. "First, we'll check out the house, then we'll meet with Mr. Grumps." She smiled at Talia and waved as they headed to the door. "Thanks for your help!"

CHAPTER 24

Rupert unlocked the door to the house on West 7th Street and stepped aside to let Kathy and Steven enter.

"Thanks for doing the showing on such short notice," Steven said.

"It got me out of the house, so I don't mind," he said with a smile. "I have to be honest, though, I was surprised to get your call. I didn't think you were interested anymore."

Kathy started looking around the living room as Steven and Rupert continued their conversation. She didn't immediately feel any bad vibes from the house, as Steven had said Samantha felt. The house was dank, depressing, and a little creepy, but nothing about it felt particularly evil.

"Well, my sister-in-law had some questions about it,"

Steven told Rupert.

The realtor nodded. "Ah. I was wondering what was going on. I try not to ask questions, but it's hard not to notice you coming with one woman on Thursday and a different woman today."

Kathy smirked as she glanced up the stairs. Light shone through the window at the top of the leaf-covered stairs. She might check the whole house out later if she didn't find anything on the first floor, but for now she wanted to wait for Steven and Rupert so as not to raise the realtor's suspicions even more.

"My wife is at home resting," Steven added.

"Do you know anything about the house?" Kathy asked Rupert. "About the history?"

"I'm afraid not," he said. "I could look into it, but I would probably only be able to get you information from the tax rolls over the past couples years and, as I understand it, it's been abandoned for much longer than that."

She made a face. If Rupert couldn't give them any more insight into what had gone on in the house and the types of people who used to live here, it would be nearly impossible to figure out what was going on with Samantha. She turned to Steven. "You said the only time you were apart from Samantha in this house was when you went down to the basement?"

Steven nodded. "It was just me and Rupert who went down."

"And where was Samantha while you two were downstairs?"

He looked back to the realtor and shrugged. "In the kitchen, I guess."

"Hmm." She stepped into the kitchen, where the basement door sat open. She could see scratches on the inside and stepped toward it to take a closer look.

"We noticed that on our way up," Rupert said. "I think it might've been a dog or something."

Kathy knelt down to inspect. "No, this isn't from a dog—or a cat. Look at the angle of the scratches. If it were an animal, they'd be more up and down. They'd be lifting their paw straight up and bringing it right now, not side-to-side. Not even a little."

"Samantha said the basement made her feel uneasy," Steven said.

"Did she say if anything happened while she was up here by herself?"

Steven shook his head.

"She found a photo while we were downstairs," Rupert chimed in. "I believe it was one of the families who used to live here."

"Do you still have it?" she asked.

The realtor stepped over to the cupboard on the opposite wall and removed the framed photo.

Kathy took it from him and stared into the eyes of a family of three. They didn't look particularly happy, but then, back in those days most people didn't smile for pictures. Still, there was something about the look in their eyes that seemed to cry out for help.

This was the first time Kathy felt any kind of bad vibe in the house.

"Do you know the names of these people?" she asked Rupert.

He shook his head. "Not without doing some research, I'm afraid. I could look into it and point you in the right direction if you decide to make an offer on the house."

Kathy turned the frame over and twisted the tiny brackets holding the backing in place. With gentle fingers, she pulled the photo out of the frame and slid it into her jacket pocket. "I'll return it after I hit up the library," she told Rupert with a smile.

That seemed to pacify the worried look growing on his face.

She turned back to Steven. "Was there anything out of the ordinary in the basement when you looked?"

He shrugged. "It's a creepy basement in an old house. It needs updating. There's obviously been wildlife getting in and out of here for years, but otherwise it just seemed like a basement."

Kathy stared at the scratches on the basement door.

"What are you thinking?" Steven asked.

"Well, if Samantha didn't want to go into the basement, then it must've been a pretty strong feeling she was getting," Kathy explained. "As we both know, she doesn't scare easily."

"No, she doesn't."

"So I'm thinking that the basement must've been a source of pain for someone—or something—and they only attached themselves to Samantha because she was the one who *wasn't* invading their space. At least, that's my theory."

"Are you two talking about ghosts?" Rupert asked. "I can assure you, there has been no indication that this house is haunted. As you know, realtors are required to disclose such information and I can proudly say that there have been no reports of any…*supernatural* entities here."

Probably because nobody's stayed in the house long enough, Kathy thought. Instead, she offered him a friendly smile.

"Would you like to see the rest of the house?" Rupert asked when neither of them responded to his comment about ghosts.

"No thanks," Kathy said. "I think I have all I need. Thanks again for showing us the house."

They walked out and Rupert locked the door behind them. Steven followed Kathy back to Samantha's car and they both waved to Rupert as he drove off.

"Are we headed to that medium's house now?" Steven checked his watch. "It's about ten o'clock."

Kathy nodded. "Hopefully that leaves us enough time." She looked up at the house, her mind racing with possibilities of everything that could've happened there. She tried to picture it back when the family from the photograph lived there. What did the neighborhood look like? Did the family have any friends? What did they think of them? Most importantly, what happened here that was so traumatic?

"What are you thinking?"

She pulled the photograph out of her pocket and looked at the faces of the family again. "I'm just worried that we don't have enough to solve this puzzle before it's too late."

CHAPTER 25

Kathy waited on the front porch of Clarence's "studio" as Steven parked his car on the street. The neighborhood had gone through rough times. Next door to the so-called studio was an empty warehouse with an oversized parking lot filled with rusted out cars that had probably been off the road for twenty years or more. There were cracks in the sidewalks and virtually no street trees. And while many of the houses were intact on the east end of the street, the west end was virtually empty, with only a few skinny houses remaining, further showcasing a neighborhood that had once been.

"This isn't exactly what I was expecting," Steven said as he joined her on the porch.

"After talking to him on the phone, I can't say I'm

surprised." Kathy raised her fist and knocked on the door three times.

At eye-level, a metal slot slid open abruptly and a wrinkled red face appeared, framed by curling white hair. "Yeah?" he grunted.

"Hi, I'm Kathy and this is Steven," she said. "I talked to you on the phone."

"The rude one, huh?"

Kathy hooked an eyebrow, but didn't say anything. After a moment of staring at each other through the slot, the opening slid shut and the lock turned in the door.

Steven looked at Kathy. "Do we just go in?"

She shrugged. "I guess so."

Opening the door, they stepped in and blinked at how dark it was. And how badly it smelled of cigarettes and incense and mildew.

"I'm in the studio!" Clarence called from around the corner. "Shut the door and lock it behind you!"

When the door was shut, Kathy could better see the room. It had obviously once been a very regal house, with an oak staircase leading upstairs and a hallway leading down to the kitchen. To the right was the parlor, which included the first floor level of the turret and its round walls.

The unique architecture did nothing to bring in more light, though. Every window had been covered with black-out curtains, requiring several small lamps to be lit around the room, despite the early-morning hour. There were bookshelves haphazardly painted white that were crammed with books and knickknacks.

There was a beat-up green couch against the far wall and a rickety desk lined with stained boxes in the circular part of the room. Clarence's husky form was curled over it, leafing through a book. Opposite the desk were two aluminum lawn chairs. He waved at them, indicating that they should sit.

"This is cozy," Steven said.

Kathy elbowed him as she wrinkled her nose against the smell. It was already getting a little better—maybe she was getting used to it or maybe it was the overflowing ashtray on Clarence's desk that gave off a strong odor of nicotine.

"It's my ghost studio," the medium said proudly. "This is my home base, where I investigate potential hauntings and where I keep all of my exorcism equipment."

"So you know how to exorcise my sister?" Kathy asked.

He rolled his eyes. "Not all exorcisms are the same. You need to know what you're up against. That's why you came to me, isn't it?"

"I just want to help my wife," Steven said. "I don't really care how it's done."

Clarence leaned back in his seat, resting his folded hands on the top of his belly. "Go on, then. Let's hear why you think this woman is possessed."

"Well, she and Steven went to look at this old house," Kathy said. "I guess she had a bad vibe about it and ever since then she's been acting weird. Snippy, grumpy, all around negative. And the bruises! Steven's been getting beat up at night—"

The medium held up his hand. "Hold on a second! Let's back up to the house. How old would you say it is?"

Kathy looked to Steven. "I don't even know."

"The realtor told us it was built in the early 1900s," Steven said. "That could mean 1901, but it could also mean 1920. It's hard to say with the record-keeping they did back then."

"Right, right," Clarence murmured. "Were there any satanic markings painted anywhere?"

Steven shook his head. "Nothing like that."

"There doesn't have to be satanic markings for it to be haunted," Kathy said. "Something traumatic has to have happened for a spirit to linger. Depending on what it is depends on how the spirit acts in the afterlife."

Clarence ignored her and looked at Steven. "Any sign of any negativity? Broken furniture, busted walls, blood stains?"

"Not really," Steven said. "The house was basically empty."

"There were scratches on the basement door," Kathy said.

"Who saw this house, you or him?" Clarence snapped.

"We both just came from there," she said.

"But he's been there twice? Including the time with the woman in question?"

Kathy opened her mouth to begin to respond, but stopped herself. Clarence might be a jerk, but he was willing to help

Samantha and that's all that mattered. So what if he only wanted to talk to Steven?

"Yes," she said quietly.

"Then let's hear it from him, shall we?" He turned back to Steven and prompted, "What was your wife's reaction to the basement in general?"

"Well, she didn't want to go down there," Steven said. "She said the whole house gave her a bad feeling, which Kathy no longer felt when we went and saw it just now."

"Right, but we're talking about your wife, not her sister."

"Samantha didn't go down to the basement," Steven said. "The realtor and I did. It wasn't until we were on our way back up that we noticed the scratches on the door. The realtor thought it was from a dog, but as Kathy pointed out, the scratches were at an angle. An animal couldn't make those marks like that."

Kathy smiled at Steven coming to her aid in front of Clarence. It was good to know that even though she and Steven had had their ups and downs, she could still count on him.

"Samantha did find a picture, though," Steven added. "While we were in the basement. The realtor thinks it might be one of the families who lived in the house."

"Do you have it with you?" Clarence asked.

Kathy pulled it from her pocket and handed it to him.

He reached for it and immediately dropped it on his desk and slid his chair backward in a desperate attempt to put as much space between him and the photo as quickly as possible.

"What is it?" Kathy asked.

"This is bad," he said, his eyes nearly bulging out of the sockets. "Very bad!"

"What kind of bad?" Steven leaned forward to get a better look at the photo.

"There is all sorts of negative energy coming from this photo." Clarence got to his feet. He hiked up his pants before walking to the jam-packed bookshelf and grabbing a small electronic device. Back at his desk, he pointed it at the photo and it let out a high-pitched whine. "The EMF is off the charts with this."

"EMF?" Steven asked.

"Electromagnetic field," Kathy explained.

"The higher the meter, the more paranormal it is," Clarence added. "This is…" He switched off the device and sunk back in his seat, staring at the photo.

"Is it…*evil* energy?" Kathy asked.

The medium nodded. "Very much so. Very *angry* energy."

"Is it the kind of energy that can cause physical harm to someone?" Steven asked.

"Maybe. You think your wife may be possessed by this thing?"

Steven nodded. "Yeah. And the sooner we can help her, the better. Would this have any long-term effects on the baby?"

"Baby?"

"My wife is pregnant."

Clarence waved a finger at them as he looked around his desk. "This is…unique. I have to consult my books. I haven't ever encountered a possession of a pregnant woman before." He stood, again reaching for his belt and pulling up his sagging pants before stepping to the bookshelf and examining the titles. "I have to do a bit of research to see how we can safely removed this spirit without also pulling out the spirit of the child growing inside her."

Steven looked at Kathy with wide eyes. "Yes, that would be very bad."

Kathy patted his knee. "We'll figure it out. Don't worry. We always do." She looked at her watch and saw that it was ten after eleven. "Shoot. I'm later than I thought. Clarence, do you think we could meet up with you again later today? I mean, if you have research to do."

The medium simply grunted, his attention lost in the book he was flipping through.

"I don't want to wait on this," Steven said. "If this thing inside Samantha might be able to harm our baby too, I want to make sure we get it right."

Kathy nodded. She didn't disagree with him, but she could only be in so many places at once. "So what do you want to do?"

"You go and be with Samantha," he said. "I'll stay here with Clarence and figure out a plan."

She looked back at the gruff old man. "Are you sure?"

He nodded. "Positive. I need to protect my family."

"Okay," she said. "If you need anything, call the club. We'll be there in less than an hour. Good luck."

Kathy rose and stepped to the door, thanking Clarence on her way out. The old man didn't even look up as she left. She walked out and the overcast sky still seemed blinding to her after the near-total darkness of Clarence's studio.

As she pulled away, she couldn't help but worry that maybe this time they weren't going to succeed.

CHAPTER 26

- OCTOBER 1934 -

There wasn't much down in the basement to help Henry try to escape. The furnace, some piping and ductwork lined the ceiling, but mostly the basement was empty. His mother had moved down several metal shelving units that she had bought from their next door neighbor, intending to use the basement for more storage. But now those shelves were rusted and useless.

The frying pan also sat useless on the dirt floor of the basement. It had broken on its latest trip down the stairs. Henry had tried to see if he could use the handle or the pan itself to open the door, but neither part proved fruitful.

Despite living in the house his whole life, Henry had never really ventured down to the basement. There was no reason to.

Even yesterday, as he sat at the top of the stairs waiting for his father to return home, Henry hadn't left the staircase. The only reason he left now was for a distraction from his painful hunger.

It had been about a day since he had eaten. Not only did his stomach churn on itself, sending painful reminders of what Henry was being neglected of, but he could also feel his muscles weaken from lack of energy. His mind going fuzzy. His body was more lethargic, requiring more willpower to do anything. Henry figured if he was up and moving, thinking, actively trying to engage his body, then maybe he could distract himself from the hunger until his father finally let him out.

And then Henry would have to be on his best behavior so this never happened again.

If his mother was still around, she wouldn't have let this drag out as long as it had. She would've done something already. She would've protected him.

But she was gone.

Upstairs, Henry heard footsteps and he hurried back up to the top of the landing, waiting by the basement door. Through the night, he had made several deep gouges into the solid wood door using only his fingernails now that the frying pan was ruined. The monotonous movement of sliding his nails up and down was enough to keep him awake. With no food in his stomach, he was afraid of falling asleep and never waking up.

The basement door swung in suddenly, forcing Henry to take several steps back down the stairs or risk being hit in the face by the door. When he saw his father's mean gaze, he took several more steps down until he was nearly at the bottom. His father put his hands on his hips and looked down at Henry.

"What are you doing?" his father asked.

"Nothing." Henry looked up at his father, trying not to showcase just how weak he felt. He never wanted his father to know the effects this so-called "punishment" was having on him. He needed to show his strength. Show that his father couldn't control him, no matter how hard he tried. "When can I be let out?"

"When my nose heals."

"But that could take weeks," Henry said.

"You should've thought about that before you hit me." He turned to go back into the kitchen.

Out of desperation, Henry cried out, "I need to be let out now! Are you *trying* to starve me to death?"

His father rushed down the stairs, jumping down the final three steps and landing on the dirt floor of the basement, inches in front of Henry.

The boy tried to escape, but his father grabbed his chin in his fist and pushed him back against the stone foundation. Henry felt his head slam hard against the stone, the cobwebs clinging to his hair. But he kept his stare locked on his father.

"Look at me, boy! You see what you've done? You see how *violent* you can be? You're an animal! And if you think I'm letting you out of here so you can beat the shit out of someone else, then you're wrong!"

Henry said nothing. He could smell the alcohol on his father's breath, even though it was only the morning. Or so he assumed.

"You're going to stay down here as long as I say! Got it, boy?"

The boy said nothing.

His father finally turned and stomped up the stairs. Henry followed, although he kept his distance. He wasn't getting out today. He wondered how long he'd be able to survive without food.

"What about school?" It was his last-ditch effort to try to reason with a man who refused to even listen to reason. "They're going to wonder where I am if I don't show up today."

His father stood in the doorway to the kitchen, the doorknob in his hand. "Your school won't even notice if you miss just one day."

Henry saw the door begin to close and he lunged forward, stretching his hand out to stop it from shutting completely. Instead, he felt a sharp, stabbing pain in his fingers as his father slammed the door closed on them.

He yelled out, withdrawing his broken fingers. Instead of pain, he felt rage overpower him.

"That's what you get for not listening!" his father bellowed from the other side of the door.

Henry raced to the landing and pounded his fists on the

door. He ignored the pain, so consumed with his hatred of his father.

The door jumped from the other side as his father kicked it. "Get the hell away from the door, boy! I don't want to hear from you again until I decide to let you out!"

CHAPTER 27

Kathy was in a hurry. She had gotten home later than she had expected, which meant she only had about fifteen minutes to get ready. Luckily, she had already pulled out her outfit the night before. The trouble was, she had planned on taking a shower before getting dressed. Not time for that now.

After putting on a brown sweater and jeans, Kathy spritzed herself liberally with perfume to cover up any body odor she may have incurred since her shower earlier that morning. Her hair, however, looked greasy. It made sense since she had gone for a run earlier that morning, plus the fact that it had been about two days since she'd washed it. Again, that was something she thought she'd be able to get done before they had to leave.

POLTERGEIST

As she fussed with an up-do hairstyle that would disguise its unwashed state and still look classy enough to meet Mary's standards, the sound of scratching met her ears again.

With bobby pins held in her mouth and both hands working the hair above her head, Kathy gave cursory glances around her bedroom. At least she knew she wasn't imagining things the other night. But still, she couldn't place where the sound was coming from. It seemed to be coming from all over.

Turning back to the mirror, she did her best to ignore it. From what she and Steven had determined last night, it was coming from whatever was going on with Samantha.

The trouble was, the sound of the scratching seemed to grow louder. To the point where Kathy was unable to ignore it without help.

She stood and went over to her clock radio beside her bed and switched it to her favorite station. Janet Jackson began to sing and Kathy bopped along to the song as she finished her hair.

The scratches grew louder.

Kathy began to hum along to the song, doing her best to not let the paranormal forces overpower her and drive her insane, which she was on the verge of doing.

Then Janet's voice began to crackle and fade as white noise took over the station. Kathy stopped singing immediately and turned to the radio, staring at it in awe. That station always came through perfectly clear and now—

"Were you just singing?" Samantha asked, abruptly cutting into Kathy's thoughts.

The scratching and crackling seemed to stop as soon as she stepped in the room and Janet's voice resumed to finish the song.

"Huh? No, just humming."

"Keep your day job," the older sister said with a chuckle.

Kathy smiled and didn't offer anything else. Her day job was a touchy subject and she needed to do her best to not stir up any arguments with that evil spirit still inside Samantha.

"Are you almost ready?" she asked. "Because I feel like I've been sitting around all morning."

"Sorry." Kathy pulled the last bobby pin out from between her lips and worked it into her hair. She tilted her head in a couple different directions, inspecting herself in the mirror. She looked good. There was no way anyone would be able to tell that she needed a shower. When she turned around, she finally saw her sister. "Oh wow. You look great!"

Samantha wore a green top that flared out at her belly. "Don't sound so surprised."

"No, it's just that you've been avoiding maternity clothes for as long as possible and today you seem to be embracing it." Kathy reached for her purse and stuck in a few items of her makeup. "It's a nice change."

Samantha fussed with the hem of her shirt. "Well, don't get used to it. This damn kid is ruining my body and I'm not happy with it."

"Don't say that," Kathy said. "You're going to have a baby. I think wearing a maternity outfit is only a small price to pay for bringing life into this world."

Samantha rolled her eyes. "Easy for you to say. While I'm trying to squeeze into a pair of fat pants, you're running around town with my husband."

Kathy froze. "What?"

"Don't play dumb. I know you two went somewhere together this morning. Sure, you took two different cars and left separately, but you were both very vague about where you'd be. And where's Steven now? Still gone. Must've had to take care of the tab at the motel."

"Sam! Steven and I are *not* having an affair, if that's what you're suggesting."

"Was I only suggesting it? I guess I should've said it outright. *You're sleeping with my husband!*"

"I am not!" Kathy cried out with wide eyes. *So much for not stirring up any arguments*, she thought. "Sam, I would never do that to you. And neither would Steven. You should know that." Even though she knew her sister's words were fueled by whatever was possessing her, they still hurt Kathy to hear them.

"Then where were you?"

"Where? We, uh…um…I thought you had it all figured out? Now you're not so sure?"

"Sounds like *you're* the one who's not sure," Samantha said. "The motel thing was just a figure of speech, so to speak. I know you were at someone's house on 21st Street. Who's was it?"

Kathy put a hand on her hip and raised an eyebrow. "And how did you know that?"

"I may have performed a location ritual on the two of you."

"So you were *spying* on us?" Kathy was outraged, but another thought occurred to her: why wasn't Samantha also brain-hopping them and reading their thoughts? Perhaps whatever was controlling her didn't realize she had that power. Best to keep that secret for as long as possible.

"It's a good thing I did since you're stealing him away from me."

Kathy shook her head and tossed her purse strap around her neck. She walked around her sister and moved to the door. "I don't have time for this. We have *your* baby shower to get to that *I* helped put together."

Samantha followed her, mocking her with a high-pitched, whiny voice.

"You have everything?" Kathy asked over her shoulder. She snatched up the keys and added, "I'm driving."

"But it's my car."

"And you're in no state to—" Kathy stopped talking the moment she opened the front door and saw Jeff standing there with his fist raised to knock.

"Hi," he said with a smile.

"Jeff! What are you doing here?"

"I just came by to see if you wanted to go for lunch."

"Right now?"

He looked at his watch. "I mean, it is lunch time."

"Oh, he's cute," Samantha muttered to Kathy. "Maybe I should try to steal him like you're stealing Steven."

"Just go wait in the car!" Kathy snapped. When Samantha walked by, Kathy gave Jeff a bright smile. "Sorry about that. We're having a bit of a tiff."

"I hope I didn't interrupt anything."

"You didn't—at least not with Samantha anyway. But I'm not going to be able to go to lunch. We're actually on our way to her baby shower, which is in, like—" She grabbed his hand to read his watch. "Oh my, ten minutes! We're going to be late."

"What about afterward? Maybe a late lunch?"

Kathy thought of Steven, still with the medium. "I probably have plans after the shower."

"What kind of plans? Anything I can help with?"

"That's sweet, but..." She trailed off, seeing his smile begin to falter as she began to turn him down. "You know what? Why don't you come to the Lawrence Park Golf Club around two-ish. You can help us clean up and then maybe you and I can sneak off somewhere afterwards."

Hopefully we'll have gotten that evil spirit out of Samantha by then, she thought.

"That sounds—"

They both jumped at the sound of a car horn. Kathy

looked over and saw Samantha irately gesturing from the passenger seat.

"I have to go," she said. "I'll see you later then?"

"You can count on it."

She leaned up and kissed him on the cheek. "I'll see you later!" She pulled the door closed behind her and raced to the car to stop Samantha's insistent honking.

CHAPTER 28

The old city directories sat open on Clarence's desk. Steven flipped through them, careful not to damage any of the pages. They were looking for the address of the house Steven and Samantha had toured. The listing would include the resident, their address, and the occupation of the resident. For Erie, the directory also included the names of the other residents at each address, which meant that Steven and Clarence would be able to determine if someone had died by looking at multiple directories.

Clarence had copies of the city directories from 1900-1950, missing only a few of them. They were stashed in a spare bedroom upstairs and Steven had the unfortunate job of retrieving them for the old man. He had been displeased to see that the upstairs was just as cluttered as the downstairs was.

Steven blinked his eyes as he turned the pages of the 1934 city directory. They had been drying out from staring so long.

"Nothing in this one." Clarence tossed the 1933 book onto his desk. Brittle pieces of paper flew up into the air. The medium leaned back in his chair and rubbed his face with his hands, running them up into his hair.

"I'm not having much luck in this one—oh, wait a minute. What was the address again?"

They had written it down to remember before they began scanning every address in the city over and over again.

Clarence searched for the small piece of paper he had somehow already lost on his desk in the half hour since they had written it down. Finally, under a pile of three different directories, he found the yellow slip. "Ah, here it is. Um, let's see. Uh…615 West 7th Street."

Steven tapped the spot in the directory with his finger. "This is it."

"Let me see." Clarence came around the desk, standing over Steven's shoulder. His halitosis struck Steven immediately.

"The Powel family," Steven read aloud. "Ivan, Helen, and Henry. Ivan was a day laborer at the Erie Metal Company. That doesn't tell us anything."

Clarence held up a finger as he walked back around the desk. He looked for the 1935 directory and flipped it open, searching for the right page. "Here we are. Hmm, interesting."

"What?" Steven held his book in his lap as he leaned forward and tried to see what the medium was looking at.

"In 1935, we have only the father listed."

"What happened to the wife and the son?"

"You're making assumptions about their relationship."

"It was the 1930s," Steven pointed out. "I think it's a safe assumption."

"Does it list any other resident at that address? During the Depression, people would often take in boarders for extra income."

Steven glanced back at the page. "No. They're the only ones. What does it mean if only Ivan is listed in 1935? Did the other two die?"

"Probably." Clarence reached for another directory. "Knowing what we know based on your experience with that house, I think it's safe to say that the death was the result of some sort of trauma. Suicide, nasty illness, murder…"

"Murder? The houses in that neighborhood are pretty close. A neighbor would've heard if someone had been murdered."

Clarence shrugged. "It was a different time back then." He pointed to the book. "Now *this* is really interesting. In 1936, that address isn't listed."

"What does that mean?"

"It was vacant."

Steven's eyes grew wide. "Man, Rupert wasn't kidding when he said the house has been sitting empty for a while."

The medium ignored him. "The fact that the whole family died within a year's time means a tremendous amount of tragedy happened in that home."

"Wait a minute. We're assuming that they all died. What if only Helen and Henry died? Maybe after that, Ivan moved away because it was just him."

"Could be," Clarence admitted. "But if I'm right, that means this wasn't a happy home. Not for a long time. And if these years—" He indicated the directories they held open. "—were the breaking points, then how long did the unhappiness linger in that house before it came to blow?"

"What do you mean?"

"Say the wife had been sick with cancer and they watched her slowly die over the course of several years. Or maybe the father was an alcoholic, smacking them around when he came home. Or the boy was a cripple, bringing financial strain and resentment to the parents. The longer the negative feelings had to fester in that house, the more negative energy the house had to pick up."

"You're saying the house *held on* to that energy?" Steven hooked an eyebrow, skeptical.

"That's exactly what I'm saying. Houses act as shells, reflecting back the energy put out by its occupants. Now, it takes years and years for these energies to manifest. Ordinarily, no family lives in one house long enough to make any serious impact, but in this case, the Powels may have been the last significant occupants. So their energies continued to linger, even after they were gone."

"And you think this negative energy somehow attached itself to Samantha?"

He nodded. "Yes, that's exactly what I believe."

"But why her? Why not me or Rupert? We were both there at the same time." He wondered if it was because his wife was a witch. But then wouldn't she have sensed the danger coming? She was certainly uncomfortable in that house, but if she had sensed danger, she would've insisted on none of them entering the house.

"It's hard to say," Clarence said. "We need more information about what happened in that house. Information that I do not have here with me. All I know is, something bad has attached itself to your wife. And according to that photograph you brought from the house, I can assure you, something bad happened there around 1934."

CHAPTER 29

Despite his efforts, Henry faded in and out of consciousness all day. His father had left for work again, leaving him alone in the basement to focus only on his hunger and his throbbing fingers. And they were certainly broken. But to an extent, he was grateful for the injury. The pain was the only thing keeping him from succumbing completely to unconsciousness that the hunger would bring.

He lay collapsed on the small landing at the top of the stairs. His thoughts were minimal. It cost too much energy to think about much. But when he did, he thought of his mother.

None of this would've happened if she were still alive.

Of course, she might've been the one locked down in the basement instead of Henry. But he would've let her out. Maybe they could've created a plan to escape. She would've known what to do. She wouldn't have let this continue.

So why was he?

The thought occurred to him so suddenly. It was so simple and yet so profound.

Why was he enduring this torment at the hands of his father when it was assuredly something that his mother never would've allowed?

He needed to change it.

He needed to make her proud.

He needed to at least *try* to escape.

Henry sat up, his head rushing from the exertion, his vision momentarily going dark. When his vision returned, he looked around and truly saw for the first time the situation he was in.

He was sleeping in a dank room with cobwebs and dirt and musk and allowing himself to be deprived of the things he needed in order to live. To survive.

That changed now.

If the house was empty, that meant that no one would see him escape. He could run across the street, go to Mrs. Johnson's house and she would keep him safe. And feed him.

Henry examined the door. It had a sizable gap around the edges. So much so that he thought he could pry it open, despite the slide lock up toward the top.

With no tools to use, he worked his fingers along the side of the door as best he could, pulling and scratching at it, trying to get it to budge. No matter how hard he tried, it wouldn't move.

Using the hand with his broken fingers, he pulled on the doorknob and saw it pulled in the loose doorjamb. The strike plate had long ago fallen off, leaving the wood exposed to deteriorate with each use of the door.

With that to his advantage, he worked the other hand toward the edge of the door. He managed to squeeze one finger in, then another, grunting at the pain as his fingers were pinched.

Finally, he couldn't take it anymore and he pulled his hand away, bringing his fingers to his mouth to nurse them.

He needed a tool. Something to wedge behind the door so he could put more effort into yanking open the door. The basement was mostly empty except…

He rushed down the stairs, driven by a new sense of hope. The metal shelving unit his mother had brought downstairs. If he could break off one of the supports, maybe he could wedge it into the door and use it as leverage to pop the door open.

At the bottom of the stairs, Henry grabbed ahold of the shelf and smashed it against the stone foundation. It clanged loudly and bent a little, but didn't break apart. He hit it again. And again. And again.

After several swings, he bent over on his knees, gasping for air, feeling his mind go fuzzy. He was exerting himself too much. Maybe so much so that he wouldn't have the strength to run across the street to Mrs. Johnson's house.

But there was no other choice.

Lifting the shelf again, he swung it against the stone foundation over and over until something broke off of it.

Except, it wasn't what he was expecting.

Instead of the side support breaking off, one of the flat metal shelves came off and clanged on the dirt floor. Henry stared at it and considered. It was better than nothing and worth a shot. Certainly, it was thinner than the support would be and would be able to slide into the crack in the door easier.

He snatched it up and raced up the stairs, working the metal between the doorframe and the door. With the hand with the broken fingers, he yanked on the door as he pushed against the metal, putting pressure on the doorjamb.

At first, it seemed as if his plan wasn't going to work.

And then it finally gave, the door nearly colliding into his face and the metal shelf crashing down the stairs in a thunderous roar.

For a moment, Henry stared at the open door, his jaw hanging open. The fresh air he felt from the kitchen was a familiar sensation that he hadn't realized he had missed.

Henry stepped into the doorway and eyed up the cabinets across the room. He doubted there was any food in there, but he was so hungry. Besides, his first priority needed to be getting out of there as fast as he could.

He rushed upstairs, pulling his book bag out of the closet and turning it over. His books and pencils spilled all over the floor. From the dresser, he grabbed fistful of clothes and stuffed them in his bag, wincing when he bumped his sensitive fingers.

Satisfied that he had enough, Henry slung the bag over his shoulder and raced down the stairs, coming to a stop on the last step.

His father had just walked through the door.

The two stared at each other, without a word. Henry's heart raced with anticipation of what was about to happen. He couldn't just sit there and let it happen. He needed to do something.

The room whipped by him as Henry raced to the back door. He was moving as fast as he could, but his father was faster. Bigger. Stronger.

Henry was about to reach for the doorknob of the back door when he felt himself being pulled backward by his backpack. He slipped out of it and dropped hard to the kitchen floor, ready to scramble to his feet.

His father was in his face before he could even think about getting up.

Grabbing a fistful of his shirt, his father dragged him back to the basement. Henry kicked his feet and struggled against his father's force, but after days without food his body was weak. He tried to grab the doorframe as he reentered the basement, but with a jerk, his father was able to yank away his hold.

With hatred burning in his father's eyes, Henry was tossed down the stairs again, the result of the scuffle in the kitchen leaving the boy too weak to grab ahold of the railing like he had in the past.

All the way down, his head smashed against the steps and the railing until he landed flat on his back on the dirt floor. His head was spinning and his body was exhausted.

As he heard the slow steps of his father descending the staircase, Henry convinced himself to get up. All he wanted to do was lay there and recoup, but there was no time. He needed to get up and try to escape.

For his mother.

When he stood, he saw something begin to flood his vision. Then he noticed how the warm blood felt on his forehead. Cupping the wound with one hand, Henry cleared his vision enough to stare his father down.

"After all I've done for you," his father muttered as he came down the last of the stairs, yanking at his belt to free it from his waist.

Henry backed up until he couldn't anymore. He was pinned against the stone foundation.

"I've been busting my ass to make sure you have a place to sleep. To put food on the table. And how do you repay me? By breaking my nose. And then I was going to let you out today, but to my surprise you were about to leave. Probably run off to that bitch of a neighbor and have her call the cops on me and waste *my* time sitting in jail overnight." He snapped his belt together, then slapped it hard against Henry's arm.

The boy recoiled and searched for an escape route. The metal shelving lay in pieces to his right and to his left was the stone wall of the coal cellar.

"You weren't ever grateful," his father went on. "You and your mother both. At least she had the decency to go and die and get the hell out of my life."

The mention of his mother enraged Henry. But he was trapped and had no energy to do anything. So he spit in his father's face with what little saliva was left in his mouth.

The belt struck his face so hard that Henry thought it might draw blood. Then another strike. And another. Now he knew he was *definitely* bleeding.

"You disrespectful little *bastard*!" his father bellowed.

Again and again the leather belt struck Henry's face until he let out a moan of pain that escaped his lips before he had a chance to even stop himself.

"Does this hurt, boy? This is what you asked for! When you thought you could run away, this is what you knew was coming! You did it to yourself!"

Henry had sunk to the ground, but when his father took a break from the beatings, he used the last of his strength to drive his fist into his father's groin.

The man yelped out, backing away from Henry and reached between his legs to cup his injured manhood.

The boy used the stone wall to help lift himself to his feet, but he was weak. His energy was gone. He didn't think he'd even be able to make it up the stairs, let alone through the house and across the street.

This is where it ended for him. If he was going to make his mother proud, he was going to go out fighting.

Henry had barely gotten his feet under him when he felt his father's thick, calloused hands around his throat.

"Let me tell you something, boy! You listen to *me*, you got that?"

Slam!

The back of Henry's head struck hard against the stone wall.

This truly was the end for him and all he could think about was his hatred for his father.

Slam!

How the man had used his position, his strength, and his age to his advantage. How, instead of protecting Henry, he abused him.

Slam!

Treated him like a slave. Like a piece of garbage to put out at the curb at the end of the week.

Slam!

Again and again, his father banged his head against the stone wall, only fueling Henry's resentment burning in his belly.

This was the end of his life, but it wouldn't stop him from getting revenge. Even as the final blow cracked Henry's skull and the light faded from his eyes, the hatred lingered. Like a ball of fury that survived even when Henry's body didn't.

This may have been the end of his life, but it wasn't the end of his story.

CHAPTER 30

Why the hell would I need a diaper service?" Samantha barked at her friend Lynette after she opened an envelope informing her of a year's service, paid in full.

"Sam," Kathy said cautiously from beside her. She had been bringing over the gifts to open while Mary snapped pictures.

"You think I want to *save* all those dirty diapers until someone comes and takes them?" she snapped. "That's disgusting!"

"It's reusable and it's good for the environment," Lynette said in a small voice.

"Do you think I give a shit about the environment? I don't want my house smelling like baby poop! How about I store the used diapers at your house? How's that sound?"

"Thank you, Lynette," Kathy said loudly. "That was very thoughtful. Wasn't that *thoughtful* of her, Sam?"

"Yeah, yeah. Thanks, I guess." She turned and looked at the other gifts. "I hope what everyone else brought is better than that."

Kathy mouthed *I'm sorry* to Lynette and made a mental note of yet another person to apologize for Samantha's actions. The list had grown to be quite a few people. This behavior was exactly why she wanted to get whatever was possessing Samantha out of her before the shower, but clearly that didn't happen.

Lynette's husband came up and took the discarded envelope to put in the trash. He had been playing golf and decided to stick around the shower after his game, leaving him as the only man in the room. Kathy could tell it made him uncomfortable, even if he didn't say anything.

Samantha only made things worse.

"What the hell do you think you're doing?" she asked him, loud enough for the whole room to hear. "What if I change my mind and decide to use that crappy service later?"

"Sam, I have the certificate here," Kathy said. "He just took the envelope."

"Why is he even here? I thought this was a female-only thing? Or is there something you need to announce?"

"Sam!" Kathy swatted at her leg. "That's enough. Do you need a break?"

POLTERGEIST

The older sister rolled her eyes, then got up and moved to the buffet table. "I need a snack."

Again, Kathy turned back to Lynette and her husband. "I'm so sorry. She's not having a good day today. I guess those hormones are really going crazy." She laughed to try to lighten the mood.

"If she doesn't like the gift, we can see about getting our money back and getting something—"

Kathy shook her head. "Nonsense. I'll talk to her and—"

"Where the hell did all the cheese go?" Samantha barked from the buffet. "I want to put cheese on my ice cream!"

Kathy jumped to her feet and rushed to her sister's side. "Sam, you're being incredibly rude."

"Well, this is my party, isn't it?"

"That doesn't mean you can—" She stopped short when she heard the sound of the scratching again. *Not here!* she panicked.

"Samantha!" Mary said in a loud whisper. "Your behavior is unacceptable! It is an embarrassment to me and your sister and all of your guests!"

"Please, just—"

All around the room, the speakers gave off terrible feedback, squealing loudly and breaking off conversations throughout the room. Everyone looked around. The microphone sat untouched in the corner, still on its stand.

"Who's touching the mic?" Mary bellowed before walking off in search of the culprit.

Kathy had an idea of what was causing the electronic malfunction.

"Come here." She put her arm around her older sister and shuffled her off to the side. "Can you try to be at least *a little* more grateful when you open these gifts?"

"What do you want me to do?"

"Be nice! Smile! Say 'thank you'!"

Samantha curled her lip. "Since when did you become the big sister?"

The scratching continued in Kathy's ear, which only added to the annoyance of Samantha's attitude. "Since you started acting like a baby!"

"What is that noise?" someone behind them asked.

"It sounds like squirrels on the roof or something," another woman said with a chuckle.

"Can we get someone to check this out?" Mary barked at an employee of the golf club. "Everything's going screwy around here and ruining the mood!"

Kathy looked around, wide-eyed. *Oh no! Other people are hearing it too! Whatever is possessing Samantha is getting stronger. It might even be tapping into her powers.*

"Just go and be nice," Kathy demanded of Samantha. "If you can't do that, then maybe we need to end this early."

Another eye roll, but Samantha said, "Fine. I'll try to play nice. Happy?"

Not in the least, Kathy thought to herself.

CHAPTER 31

The microfilm machine was something that Steven thought he'd never have to use again. It was a relic from college that he had been glad to put behind him. Yet as he sat at the Erie Public Library, scrolling through old newspaper records from the 1930s, he couldn't help but note the irony.

"Slow down!" Clarence barked beside him. "How can you even read the dates if you scroll through that fast?"

The medium had insisted on coming with Steven. They were on the hunt for an obituary or death notice of Helen Powel, the mother. All they knew was that she had died sometime between 1934 and 1935, which meant that they needed to look through daily newspaper records for both years.

"Give me that!" Clarence tried to take control of the dial,

which navigated which part of the microfilm reel was displayed.

Steven shrugged him off. "I've got it!" He stared at the page and noted a small notice in the corner. "I just found the wife's death notice."

Clarence leaned in closer than was comfortable for Steven, but he was quiet as they both read the brief entry.

HELEN M. POWEL - MRS. HELEN POWEL (34), WIFE OF IVAN POWEL, AND MOTHER OF HENRY POWEL, PASSED AWAY THURSDAY, OCTOBER 11TH AFTER SUFFERING A SEIZURE IN HER HOME. MRS. POWEL IS THE DAUGHTER OF THOMAS AND GERTRUDE (BURNS) SMITH. FUNERAL SERVICES WILL BE HELD AT BURTON FUNERAL HOME ON OCTOBER 13TH AT 10 O'CLOCK.

"Well," Clarence said once he'd finished. "That doesn't tell us much."

"Do you think the poltergeist is Helen?" Steven asked.

He shook his head. "Not enough information to determine that yet. You find anything on the husband or the son?"

Steven began to scroll through and was surprised to see the Powel name pop up again only two weeks later.

"It's another death notice," he told the medium. "For the son."

Poltergeist

"The *boy* died?" Again, the medium leaned in too close to read over Steven's shoulder.

Henry I. Powel - Henry Powel (10), passed away at his home at 615 West 7th Street on October 29th. There will be a short memorial service at Erie Cemetery on October 31st.

"He was buried on Halloween?" Clarence said.

"I guess so. And no funeral?"

"Something's not right about this."

"I agree," Steven said. "Mother and son died only two weeks apart?"

"And notice how it didn't list the cause of death for the boy? Makes me wonder if he died from something they couldn't pretty-up for the newspaper."

"Like what?"

"Well, you notice how the father isn't mentioned in the death notice? Why don't you check the police blotter."

Steven was skeptical, but scrolled to the next section of the same newspaper and saw the name for Ivan Powel listed.

Ivan Powel was arrested October 29th for the murder of Henry Powel, his ten-year-old son. The senior Powel reported the death of his son, whose body was found in the basement of the Powel residence severely beaten. Ivan Powel is currently in the city jail, awaiting trail.

"Just as I thought!" Clarence said. "This bastard killed his son."

Steven stared at the notice, still shocked at what he had just read. How could someone kill their child? He thought about the baby in Samantha's belly. Even though he hadn't actually laid eyes on them, he knew that no matter what, he'd want to protect them.

"So it wasn't a happy home," Clarence went on. "And that confirms my theory that it's a poltergeist possessing your wife."

"So what does that mean? How do we get it to leave?"

The old man leaned back in his chair and rested his hands on his belly as he thought. "You said she's pregnant?"

Steven nodded.

"And you're the father?"

"As her husband, I would certainly hope so."

"Have you had any injuries lately?"

"Like a broken bone or anything?"

Clarence hook his head. "Not even that serious. Anything at all."

"I've had some bruises and a couple bloody noses."

The medium smiled. "Aha!"

"What does that mean?" Steven was growing frustrated. He needed to be careful to keep his voice down in the quiet library.

"I think the poltergeist is the little boy."

"Henry? You think a ten-year-old is possessing my wife?"

"His spirit is much older than that, but still carries the anger and the hatred of his ten-year-old body."

Steven shook his head. He was tired of these half-answers. He wanted definitives. "What does that even mean?"

Clarence sighed, annoyed. "Henry is the poltergeist, right? His spirit lingered in that house—the house he died in and the one you and your wife entered. So when you and the realtor went down into the basement, the place where he died, he must've sought refuge in your wife."

"Why her? Why not me or Rupert?"

"She was the only one who wasn't disturbing his final resting place," Clarence said. "*And* I think that he could sense that she was a mother—or about to become one, depending on how you look at it."

"And the bruises and nosebleeds I've been getting?"

"Think about it…"

"Because I'm the father?"

Clarence nodded. "Clearly this poltergeist has daddy issues. I mean, wouldn't you if your father killed you?"

The sentence was so obscure and yet made perfect sense. He wondered how many people around them could hear their conversation, but at the moment he didn't care much.

"What about the scratches we've been hearing?" he asked.

Clarence waved a finger. "Ah! With that, I believe it's because we're looking at a powerful poltergeist here. He's had more than fifty years to let his anger fester and boil to the point where he could possess someone. Most poltergeists are stuck to the places where they died."

"So Kathy and I have been hearing the scratches as a side effect of the power this thing has?"

"Exactly. Wouldn't be surprised if it were electronics too. TVs, radios, those sorts of things."

Makes sense with what I've noticed, Steven thought.

"But…how can you be sure that *this* is the poltergeist we're looking at?" he asked. "Maybe something else happened in the house that was bad that caused another poltergeist?"

Clarence shook his head. "Back at my studio, when we were looking through the city directories, I saw that the house had been empty up until two years ago. And your realtor told you that they didn't own it for long. Nobody else has lived in that house since the Powel family. That tells me that it's haunted."

"Not anymore, if the thing that was haunting it followed us home." Steven rewound the microfilm and ejected it. His hands shook as he tried to put the reel back in its container to return to the circulation desk. "I need to get to the golf club to tell Kathy. We need to do something about this."

POLTERGEIST

Clarence stood and put his hand on Steven's shoulder to steady him. "And we will. But if we're going to perform an exorcism, there are some things we need to get first."

CHAPTER 32

- OCTOBER 1935 -

Ivan Powel sat in his living room, enjoying a beer after work. It was the one year anniversary of his son's death, but that wasn't on Ivan's mind. Instead, he was enjoying his freedom. He was finally alone. Nobody to tell him what to do, or get in his way, or disrespect him.

Months ago, the charges against him for Henry's murder were dropped. An error in the schedule at work meant that his boss ended up incorrectly vouching for him, saying that Ivan had been working late that night.

With that alibi, police determined that they had found Ivan covered in Henry's blood because he had attempted to resuscitate the boy. The case was officially still ongoing, but with no new leads and no one pushing for the police to continue to search for a killer, Henry Powel's murder had been put into the cold case pile.

The only hiccup to Ivan's rediscovered freedom was his hearing. He must've damaged it in the last couple weeks because he'd been hearing scratching of some sort. It had been going on for at least two weeks, only getting worse every day. It wasn't too much of a bother, so he mostly ignored it. He found that he didn't seem to hear it if he was drunk.

Ivan finished off his beer and got to his feet to retrieve another one from the refrigerator.

After he took the last bottle out of the fridge, he noticed, out of the corner of his eye, one of the cabinets bouncing closed. As if someone had just released it.

Ivan stepped forward and inspected the cabinet. He glanced around the kitchen for any signs of anyone in the room. There were none. Turning back to the cabinet, he opened it and peered inside. Maybe there was a critter or something that he needed to lay traps for.

Inside, all he saw was the family picture Helen had insisted on years ago. When Ivan was first released from jail after the charges were dropped, he couldn't bare to look at it so he stashed it in the cabinet and had completely forgotten about it since. Now, he stared into the eyes of the woman who had been his wife and the little boy who had been his son. A strange feeling overcame him.

Guilt.

Quickly, he stashed the frame back in the cabinet and retreated back to the living room so he could listen to his favorite radio show.

Before he left the kitchen, however, he heard the cabinet door slam shut behind him again.

Ivan whirled around, expecting to find an intruder. He suspected Mrs. Johnson or some other neighbor who didn't hide the fact that they thought he was responsible for Henry's death. Maybe they had come to deliver their own sense of justice.

Instead, Ivan saw no one in the dark kitchen.

Out of precaution, he opened one of the drawers and retrieved his revolver. If anyone did break in, he was well within his rights to shoot them dead.

With gun in hand, Ivan went back to his chair and took a sip of his beer. The radio show began, but the annoying scratching sound in his ears intensified. Ivan turned up the dial on the radio's volume, but it only added to the noise.

The scratching wouldn't relent.

At the front of the house, the windows slid open, sending the fall chill inside. Ivan set his gun down and jumped up to shut them, but every time he pulled them back into place and locked them, they would unlock and slide back up again.

He backed away and snatched his gun from the table. He was losing his mind.

In the kitchen, the cabinet doors began to open and shut on

their own again, followed by the basement door banging open and closed.

The basement.

He hadn't brought himself to go down into the basement since…

This was a dream. A horrible nightmare. That's all this was. If he just—

Ivan flinched, feeling a sharp pinch in his arm. Then another. And another. There was no one else in the room, yet someone—or some*thing*—was pinching him.

And then the chills started.

These were separate from the cold wind blowing in through the windows. This chill went right down to his bones, as if he were standing out in a blizzard with nothing on.

Ivan began to rub his arms to try to warm himself up, but his hand recoiled as soon as it touched his own skin. His eyes widened when he looked down at his arms.

Bruises. Up and down both arms.

At the same time, his nose began dripping blood, staining all down the front of him. Ivan couldn't make it stop.

The door. He could leave. Whatever was happening was happening in this house. So if he went outside—

He turned the knob, but the front door wouldn't budge.

The windows.

Ivan ran to the windows, pushing aside the furniture to get to them. He leaned over to start to crawl through, but the window slammed shut on him. Then the next one down did. And the next. One by one, each window slid closed with a bang, trapping Ivan inside.

Then the radio started. At first, only the volume grew, then it began shrieking, as if the radio were tuned to the wrong frequency.

He put his hands over his ears and shouted: "What the hell is going on!"

Suddenly, the power cut out—lights, radio, everything was quiet and still. Ivan spun around, lowering his arms and trying to catch sight of anyone lurking outside. He raised his revolver with a shaky hand and pointed it at the windows, but didn't see any movement.

Then, directly in front of him, a faint figure in white appeared.

Ivan backed away until he was pressed up against the wall. The figure was short and small. It almost resembled—

No, it couldn't be.

That was impossible.

Just as quickly as it appeared, the figure was gone. But the memory still lingered on Ivan's mind.

Henry.

His son.

Suddenly exhausted, Ivan sunk back into his chair. The electric kicked on again, the radio only playing static, the lights began to flicker. Meanwhile, the doors and windows opened and closed over and over again.

"Stop it!" Ivan screamed, but the terror continued. He felt the chill again, striking him suddenly. It felt as if he would never be warm again. Like his body had lost its ability to heat itself.

And the scratching. The noise had intensified to the point where Ivan could hear nothing else. He sunk to the floor and lowered his head into his lap, forgetting that he still gripped his revolver in his hand. A thought occurred to him as he studied the gun.

There was only one way out of this madness.

He raised the gun.

And squeezed the trigger.

CHAPTER 33

Thankfully, the baby shower had finally ended. Kathy sat on a chair, exhausted, near the windows overlooking the golf course as the caterers came in and began to clean up. Samantha seemed to be in a better mood, now that she was alone and left to peruse her gifts without interruption.

"Well, I think that went okay," Mary said from beside Kathy. "Samantha seemed a little, um, well, she seemed a little *tired*. That's all. I'm sure the guests all understood."

Kathy nodded, only half listening. She felt as if she had just spent the day watching a toddler. Drained physically, mentally, and emotionally. She only hoped that Steven was finding enough with Clarence to finally put an end to Samantha's moodiness.

At least, her supernatural moodiness.

"I do hope the men arrive soon to help us clean up," Mary said. "Did you call Steven? Tell him that we're ready?"

The prolonged silence told Kathy that Mary had been talking to her and she quickly sat upright. "What? Oh, Steven is busy running errands this morning. I'm not sure whether he'll be here or not."

"To his own wife's baby shower? Surely, I raised him better than that."

"He's getting stuff for the baby," she lied.

"Oh. Well. Still. He should be here."

"Is Marty coming?"

"Yes, he should be here anytime now." Mary glanced toward the doors. "I'll go out and see if he's here."

Kathy nodded and watched her walk away, grateful to be left alone.

The caterers were packing up their tables now, chitchatting amongst themselves.

"This is my last Saturday for a while," the taller one said to his friend.

"Yeah? How'd you manage that?" He closed up one of his plastic bins and piled it on a cart that was already filled with other bins.

"My wife has something for us to do every weekend from now until the new year." The taller one pulled a garbage bag out of the bin and tied it off.

"Yeesh, that's rough."

"What about you? You stuck in the Saturday cycle?"

"Yeah, I've got a few more lined up. They're not too bad. Like today, I still have most of the day left. I'm going to take my son to the batting cages one last time before the winter comes."

Kathy watched as Samantha snapped to attention, her eyes locked on the shorter man. In horror, she watched as her older sister reached for the pair of scissors she had been using to cut into boxes and charged at the men.

Swinging her hands up, Kathy froze the room and called for her sister, just as Samantha was raising the scissors above the man's head.

"Sam!"

The older witch's concentration broke and she turned to look at Kathy, who used the opportunity to knock the scissors out of her hand. They clattered to the floor.

Kathy, meanwhile, pulled on her sister's arm and led her to the storage closet, which was the only private place she could think of nearby.

When they were alone, she finally released her and asked, "What the hell was that?"

Samantha apparently didn't want to talk and swung her fist at Kathy, who blocked the door. Kathy did her best to fend off her sister's advances, trying not to bump her stomach in any way. It was a new challenge to a familiar routine they hadn't been through since they were little girls.

POLTERGEIST

They continued to fight, with Samantha eventually overpowering Kathy and knocking her to the floor. The younger witch struggled under her sister's hold, kicking and squirming to free herself, but it was no use. So when Samantha leaned particularly close, Kathy whipped her head forward and smacked it hard into Samantha's.

Their skulls clinked together. Kathy reached up and rubbed her forehead as the pain overwhelmed her. Samantha, meanwhile, collapsed on the floor beside her.

Hopefully being knocked unconscious doesn't hurt the baby, Kathy thought to herself.

Grabbing a chair from the stack in the corner, Kathy set it in the center of the room, then reached down to lift her sister into the chair. She could use cloth napkins to secure her in place. Hopefully that would be enough to keep her worsening attitude at bay until Steven got there.

She only hoped that he would have a plan to help Samantha.

CHAPTER 34

The door swung open into the dark, cluttered, and musty room that Clarence called his studio. The medium walked in with Steven close behind.

"I don't understand what we're doing here," Steven grumbled. "We need to get to the golf club to help Samantha and warn Kathy."

"And we will! But we're not going to go in half-cocked! We would be no help to them without the proper equipment." Clarence shuffled around papers on his desk.

"I'm going to call the club," Steven said impatiently. "See if they can put Kathy on the phone. Do you have a phone book anywhere?"

Clarence scratched his scruffy white beard and pointed to a

stack of thick yellow tomes in the corner. "There."

Many of the phonebooks in the pile were still wrapped in the plastic bags they had been delivered in. Steven guessed that every time one was dropped off on the porch, Clarence just picked it up and added it to the pile. As far as Steven could tell, nothing in this place was organized.

Taking the book off the top, Steven flipped through until he found the number for the Lawrence Park Golf Club. He grabbed the phone and dialed, meanwhile watching the old man as he tossed his own place.

"Nah, not there," Clarence grumbled to himself after he had checked the surface area of his desk. He fell back into his chair and pulled open several drawers. He produced a Zippo lighter from one and flicked it open. "Oooh, I've been looking for that! I'll need to get more oil for it, but it should be okay."

Steven waved his hand at him, signaling that he should hurry up. Part of his impatience was the busy signal he kept getting whenever he tried to call the golf club. Were they really busy or did they just not want to take any calls?

Finally, he gave up and slammed the phone back in its cradle.

"Can I help you find anything to speed this along?"

"Almost got it all." Clarence pulled a wooden cross out of a filing cabinet in the corner and stuffed it under his arm.

"What do you need the cross for? Samantha isn't possessed by a demon, is she?"

"No, a poltergeist."

"Then why the cross?"

Clarence continued to search around his clutter. "It works the same way, dispossessing people. Actually, we'll need to stop at a church somewhere and get some holy water too."

Idly, Steven wondered what that would do to his wife. He knew she wasn't evil in any sense of the word, but when they had gotten married, she had been adamant about not having the ceremony in a church. Was that her own personal feeling or was there something she wasn't telling him? Would her skin burn at the touch of holy water? Could she even step into a church?

Get a grip, he told himself. *This isn't the 1600s in Salem, Massachusetts.*

"Wait a minute, what's with that?" Steven asked Clarence as a warning. The medium had picked up a hammer and several metallic nails that reflected the light.

"These are silver nails," he explained. "When I nail it through the center of the cross, it will help ground the spirit to the earth and will take away its ability to possess."

"So it's not going to move on to the afterlife?"

Clarence chuckled. "I'm not sure *where* they go. But the way I see it is, do you really want a nasty sucker like that in *your* afterlife?"

Steven didn't have an answer. He hadn't thought much about where he'd go when he died. It was still too far off to really consider. At this point, all he knew was that he wanted his wife back before anything bad happened to her. Or their baby.

"All right, I think I'm all set," Clarence announced. "We can stop at Saint Peter Cathedral on the way."

"That's not on the way. It's a good five, ten minutes *out* of the way."

"It's a bigger church!" Clarence roared in his phlegmy voice. "Less opportunity for people to question why you need the holy water."

Steven sighed. "Okay. Fine. But hurry up."

They started to the door and as Steven stepped outside into the fall breeze, Clarence turned back.

"*Now* what?"

A minute later, the medium emerged with a bag of salt. "This is an essential. Can't believe I almost forgot it." He passed off the tools he had collected to Steven, then turned to lock the door.

"Do I even want to know what salt does?"

"It keeps a spirit contained after we expel it from your wife's body." Clarence grabbed the items from Steven's hand and followed him down the steps back to Steven's car. "When we get to Saint Pete's, there's not a lot of parking so just leave the car running. Circle the block if you have to. I'll be out as soon as I can."

Steven sighed and shifted into gear. He only hoped that they would be able to arrive in time.

CHAPTER 35

Trapping Samantha in the storage closet sounded like a good idea in the spur of the moment. But now that they had both spent a considerable amount of time in there, Kathy was running out of ways to stall.

The latest knock on the door was not unexpected. Mary had already knocked several times. "Kathy, dear, what are you girls doing in there?"

"Samantha's feeling sick," Kathy lied. "We just need some privacy."

"I assure you, everyone's left already. It's only me, Marty, and the caterers left. And we're all waiting to clean up, which we need to get into the storage closet to do."

"Samantha's keys are in my purse by the gift table," Kathy

said. "Feel free to take what you can out to the car. I would help, but…"

She looked over at her sister, who was just starting to stir. Apparently Kathy had hit her harder than she thought. Not that the throbbing of Kathy's own head had ever gone away.

Note to self: head-butting is a last resort.

Kathy had managed to tie up her sister with several cloth napkins that had been stashed in a box on one of the shelves in the storage room. She did her best to tie each one tight enough to restrain her supernaturally-charged sister.

"Do you expect us to *drive* them to your house and *unload* them there for you too?" Mary asked.

"No thanks! Steven should be here soon and he can help!"

Through the door, Kathy could hear Mary grumbling, but there was nothing she could do. What would Mary say if she saw Samantha tied up? She already thought the sisters were a little strange, not that Kathy could blame her for that.

"It's okay, Kathy," Marty said on the other side. "We'll take care of it."

Naturally, Mary began to protest. "But—"

"We'll take care of it," he said again.

Kathy began to let out a sigh of relief, but wasn't able to finish it. From behind her, Samantha began to shout incoherently.

"Kathy! What is that?" Mary called from the other side of the door.

"Are you two okay?" Marty asked. "What's going on?"

Moving quickly, Kathy tried to put her hand over her sister's mouth, but immediately regretted that decision when her sister snapped her teeth at her.

"Easy!" the younger witch shouted. She stopped short when she noticed that Samantha's eyes had gone white. No sign of her irises or pupils.

The evil spirit was taking over. Time was running out.

The doorknob began to jiggle as the Harpers tried to get in. Thinking quick, Kathy grabbed the last remaining cloth napkin and put it in Samantha's mouth like a gag. It was something that she hated to do, but at the moment, it was absolutely necessary.

Moving behind her sister, Kathy tried to tie off the napkin behind Samantha's head, but it was too short. So she had to hold it there. Worse, the gag only helped muffled the sound, not stop it.

"Kathy, you two are scaring me," Mary said. "What's going on? Does Samantha need to go to the hospital? Is something wrong with the baby?"

"Everything's fine!" Kathy struggled to keep the gag in place as her sister thrashed around.

"I'm calling for an ambulance!" Marty announced.

"No!" Kathy snapped. "No need for an ambulance! We're okay! Really! Samantha's just, um…letting off some steam!"

If ever there was an award for the worst lie in human

history, that probably would've been it, Kathy thought to herself. *Steven better hurry up!*

CHAPTER 36

"Would you slow down!" Clarence wheezed behind Steven. He limped up the path to the front door of the golf club.

Steven turned to face the medium, walking backward toward the door to keep moving. "Can't! Gotta get inside before—" As he turned back around, he nearly collided with another man who was walking in to the club. He had blond hair, wore a leather jacket, and jeans. "Sorry!"

"It's okay," the man said. "Are you here for the baby shower?"

"Sort of," Steven said. "Why?"

"I'm looking for Kathy. She said she'd be here."

Clarence finally arrived at the door, a little breathless. "What are we doing? Running a marathon? Not all of us are still in our *twenties!*"

"Sorry," Steven muttered. He turned back to the man. "Listen, Kathy is here somewhere, but I'm sure she's busy right now. And I don't mean to be rude, but I really have to go!" He raced off inside.

The blond man watched him disappear into the building.

Clarence nodded and pointed to Steven. "Irritable bowels. He never knows when it's going to hit." When he stepped inside the lobby, he muttered under his breath, "That'll show him to run off without me."

Inside, Steven saw his parents standing at the door to the storage room. Most of the tables had been stripped, except for the gift table. There were a few other people packing up crates of silverware and dishes, but it looked like everyone had already left.

Steven looked around, trying to find where else his wife could be. He saw the hallway leading to the bathrooms and the kitchen—he didn't hear anything from that direction. There was the door out onto the patio, but he could see through the windows that nobody was out there, other than golfers. That left the door marked STORAGE. That must've been where Samantha and Kathy were.

"Don't just stand there," Clarence said as he came up behind Steven. "We need to move quickly! The longer the poltergeist is in her, the stronger hold it'll have on her!"

Running up, Steven's parents met him halfway across the room.

"Do you want to tell *your* sister-in-law that it's rude to barricade herself in the closet while everyone else cleans up?" Mary asked.

At least that confirms where they are, Steven thought.

"And where have you been?" she went on. "This is a baby shower for *your* child! You should've been here right before it ended to thank everyone and help clean up!"

"I know, but—"

"Son, I'm kind of worried about Samantha," Marty said. "Kathy's been saying everything's fine, but we heard Samantha screaming just now. Before that, she hadn't said anything at all. I'm inclined to call an ambulance."

"No!" Steven blurted.

Clarence pushed by the three of them and stepped to the storage room door.

"Who's he?" Mary asked. "What's going on?"

The door opened and Clarence stepped into the closet without issue.

"Why did they let him in but not us?" she demanded. "Steven, I expect an answer!"

"I'm sorry," he said, fishing for a lie that wouldn't contradict any that Kathy might've told them. "Kathy called me and said that Samantha's not feeling well. She just wants to go home."

"Well, we would've taken her home," Marty said. "She didn't need to hide in the closet."

"Is she going into labor?" Mary asked. "It's two months

early! The survival rate for a baby that small is—she needs to go full term!"

"Please, can we have some space?" Steven pleaded. "I'll take care of everything here if you want to just go home."

"Kathy wanted us to load up the gifts into Samantha's car," Mary said.

"Don't worry about that. Just go. Please."

"Son, we're not just going to leave if something's wrong here," Marty said. "We're going to see it through."

Steven sighed. "Samantha…had…an *accident*."

"An accident?" Mary asked. "Like, she…?"

"Yes, she needs a whole new set of clothes, but I wasn't home to grab her any so she just wants to sneak out without being seen."

"Where were you if you weren't home?" Mary asked. "It's your wife's baby shower and you're out joyriding? We raised you better than that, you know!"

"Mom! Dad! Please. Just go home. This is something I need to take care of privately."

The Harpers exchanged looks. Neither of them liked the idea of leaving. But the look on their son's face showed that he was serious.

"Okay," Marty said first. "If that's what you think is best."

"You'll call us if you need something," Mary said. "If anything happens with the baby—I don't want to miss the birth of my first grandchild!"

"I'll be fine."

Slowly, the Harpers walked off, giving a regretful look back at Steven. When they crossed the room, they disappeared through the door.

As soon as they were gone, Steven went to the storage closet and knocked.

"We need a minute!" Kathy called out with an edge to her voice.

"Kathy's it's me," Steven said. "Let me in."

Without a moment's pause the closet door opened and Steven stepped into the madness.

CHAPTER 37

Kathy struggled to keep the gag in Samantha's mouth as Clarence finished laying the circle of salt around her. Samantha thrashed against her restraints in the chair, growling deep in her throat, and drooling around the gag to the point where it looked like she was foaming at the mouth.

With the salt circle having been laid, Clarence opened the door and Steven stepped in. Kathy hadn't even heard a knock or anything.

"Get out of there!" Clarence barked at her, waving his hand out of the circle.

Kathy leapt back, careful not to disturb the salt line.

"Sam!" Steven cried out.

"That's not Samantha right now," Kathy said. She could tell

by the look in her sister's eyes.

"The poltergeist has full control of her right now," Clarence added.

"Let! Me! Out!" Samantha roared in a voice that wasn't her own. It was deep, guttural, and sounded demonic.

Without hesitation, Clarence squirted a bottle of something in Samantha's face. It looked like water, but it happened so fast that Kathy couldn't be certain. Samantha recoiled from the spray as steam rose up and dissipated into the air.

"Holy water," Clarence announced to Steven and Kathy. "Now you know why I got so much of it."

"Is it hurting her?" Kathy asked.

"It's not hurting her," he said. "It's hurting the poltergeist."

"Then douse her," Steven said, keeping his eyes locked on his wife.

Clarence went to the pile in the corner where he had dropped his supplies that he had brought from his studio and retrieved the book. He flipped through the pages as Samantha continued to shout in the demented voice that wasn't her own.

"You think you can contain me?" she bellowed. "I'm unstoppable! If you destroy this vessel, I'll just move on to the next!"

The medium ignored the threats and passed the book off to Kathy and Steven. "Here. Read this passage out loud."

"It's an incantation," Kathy said as she took it from him.

He got down on his knees and reached for the cross from

the pile, as well as the hammer and the silver nails. "Both of you. Now!"

Steven looked over at Kathy. "But I'm not a—"

"Just read the damn thing!" the old man shouted as he lumbered down onto his knees. "Keep going until I tell you to stop!"

Samantha shook in her chair and slowly inched across the floor within the circle. One of the cloth napkins had come loose and her right wrist was free. Luckily, the one at the crook of her elbow still held tight so she was unable to free herself. The ones around her ankles also held.

Meanwhile, Clarence carefully crossed the salt line and crawled underneath the chair.

"Ready?" Kathy asked Steven.

He nodded.

Evil spirit, we banish thee.
From now until eternity.
Release your host, set her free.
Depart from this world, let us be.

As they recited the spell, Clarence tried to wedge himself under the chair Samantha was bound to. The poltergeist possessing Samantha had other ideas, though, and wiggled in the chair until she managed to free one leg. She used it to stomp on Clarence's hand beneath the chair.

The medium cursed loudly and recoiled. He jumped across the salt line and back to his pile of supplies.

Meanwhile, Steven and Kathy continued to recite the spell, which only seemed to agitate the evil spirit further.

Clarence grabbed the bottle of holy water and squirted it all over Samantha. She shouted out in a deep voice that was clearly a direct line right from the poltergeist.

With only half the bottle left, Clarence lifted it above his head and doused himself in the blessed water.

Kathy eyed him curiously, but kept her focus on reciting the incantation with Steven.

Samantha's attempts to free herself were increased as she broke out of another restraint. Now, she had her right arm free, which she used to swat at Clarence as he crawled back under the chair. When her arm hit him, however, she recoiled and more steam rose up as she hit his holy water-soaked clothing.

In retaliation, a mysterious wind began to circle around the room. It grew in strength, pulling at their clothing, catching the contents of the shelves lining the walls. Soon, there were paper plates, cloth napkins, cooking utensils, and more errant items flying through the air as the wind increased in strength.

Kathy and Steven huddled together, flattening out the pages of the book they held so they could both read from it—even though they had repeated the spell so many times already that they knew it by heart now.

Curiously, the salt remained in place on the floor. It seemed as if the power the poltergeist had still couldn't penetrate the salt line.

Clarence lay on the floor beneath the chair with the wooden cross, the hammer, and the silver nails. His knees were on the opposite side of the salt line and his back bent awkwardly to squeeze underneath. His belly hung out as his shirt rode up from the awkward angle, and it blew in the supernatural wind.

Soon, the door began swinging open and slamming shut, causing Kathy to jump. She quickly regained her composure and kept reading the spell with Steven. She didn't even flinch as the lights began to flicker as well.

Finally, Samantha's head rolled back and a black cloud emerged from her mouth. When it passed, the door remained still, the light stopped flickering, and Samantha's head slumped onto her shoulder.

They watched as the black cloud tried to escape, but only swirled around the room—trapped by the impenetrable salt line. It moved down toward the floor in an attempt to possess Clarence, but recoiled at the holy water still drenching his clothes.

Unsure of whether to stop, Kathy continued reciting the incantation, and Steven followed suit. They both watched wide-eyed and helpless as the spirit bounced off the invisible force field created by the salt line.

Clarence, meanwhile, used the hammer to drive a silver nail into the center of the wooden cross.

The poltergeist let out a terrible shriek—where the sound came from, exactly, couldn't be determined—and it was driven closer to the cross with each swing of Clarence's hammer, as if pulled magnetically.

The medium continued to pound the silver nail into the cross, moving methodically in the tight space. The black cloud sunk deeper and deeper, disappearing into the silver nail with each swing.

Finally, with one last swing of the hammer, the nail was flattened into the cross and the room went silent and still. Every sign of the poltergeist seemed to have disappeared in a second.

"It's over," Clarence announced, a little breathless. He grunted as he retreated from the spot under the chair, fixing his shirt as he sat back on his feet.

Steven rushed to Samantha and Kathy took a step forward, but noticed Clarence pointing through the door.

"Uh…who's that?"

Kathy turned and saw Jeff standing in the open doorway. His eyes were wide and his mouth hung slack. There was no doubt that he had seen everything.

CHAPTER 38

J eff!" Kathy called after him as she ran to catch up to him. "Wait! I can…explain…"

It didn't matter. Jeff was already through the front doors, across the parking lot, and jumping behind the wheel of his car. As Kathy pushed through the door herself and stepped into the damp, fall air, she heard him squealing his tires as he peeled out of the parking lot.

She sighed and dropped her shoulders. That was another perfectly good man she had scared away. Maybe someday she'd find a good one that she could hold on to.

Returning to the storage closet, she was happy to see that Samantha was awake. Steven knelt beside her and held her hand.

Clarence, meanwhile, picked up the cross and tossed it in the trash. "We'll want to make sure this ends up in a landfill. The closer to the ground, the better trapped the spirit will be."

Kathy ignored him and rushed to Samantha's other side. "Are you okay?"

The older sister nodded. "Tired." Her skin was washed out with deep circles under her eyes. She leaned against the back of the chair, resting all of her weight on it as she seemed unable to even keep her head up straight.

"That's from the poltergeist sharing her body," Clarence said. "And I'm sure the baby is only exasperating that. It'll be a few days before you're back to your normal self."

"Here, let's get you out of these restraints." Kathy untied the few remaining cloth napkins that still held Samantha to the chair. "Steven, see if you can get her a glass of water or something. Maybe that'll help perk her up."

Samantha seemed to be getting back to her usual self. She sat up straighter and took in her surroundings for the first time. "It was so weird. I was out of it, but I was aware of everything that was happening too."

"You remember?" Kathy asked, surprised. She had just finished releasing Samantha's arms and was working on the final restraint on her ankle.

"I'm not surprised," Clarence said. "It possessed her. It didn't kill her. It's like he took control of the reigns for a little bit, that's all."

Samantha nodded. "It felt like a bad mood at first—something I couldn't escape from. And then it just seemed to be more and more out of my control until…we got here."

"And the baby?" Kathy asked.

The older witch put a hand to her belly and breathed a sigh of relief. "It just kicked."

Kathy looked over to Clarence. "There's no way the poltergeist stuck around inside the baby, is there?"

The medium shrugged. "Can't offer you a definitive. Never seen a case where a pregnant woman was possessed before. Judging by the way the spirit was sucked into the cross, I think you're free and clear now."

"Good," Kathy said.

"Well, I'll give you two a minute," he said. "I'll be waiting in the lobby whenever somebody wants to take me home." He waddled off out of the closet, leaving the sisters alone.

Samantha watched as he left, then asked Kathy in a whisper, "Who the hell is that guy?"

Kathy looked back at Clarence, then turned to Samantha. "He's a medium Steven and I have been working with to help you."

"You and *Steven*?"

The younger sister laughed. "Yeah. He's been a big help." At Samantha's continued confusion, she added, "We'll explain everything later."

CHAPTER 39

Samantha had never been more exhausted. Even throughout her pregnancy, even when she had had very long days, the time after her exorcism trumped them all.

Right after the baby shower, she went straight to bed to take a nap. Now she was just starting to stir and she was very surprised to see that it was dark outside.

Well, she thought to herself, *it gets darker earlier now that it's almost November. Maybe I haven't slept that long.*

And then Steven walked in with his bathrobe on.

"Oh," he said with a smile. "Did I wake you up?"

She pushed herself up in bed and shook her head. "No, you didn't. How long have I been asleep?"

"Let's see, we got home around three-thirty, so I'd say

you've been asleep for about six hours."

"Six *hours!*" She turned and looked at the clock, which showed that it was just after ten. "Why didn't anybody wake me?"

"We figured you needed your rest. Are you *awake* awake now? Do you want me to stay up and chat with you for a bit?"

In truth, Samantha felt like she could probably sleep straight through the night. But there was something that had been bothering her. Something she remembered from the poltergeist's possession that bothered her. Now that she and Steven were alone, it was the perfect time to bring it up.

"Actually, there's something I need to say." She patted the bed beside her. "Sit."

He pulled his bathrobe off and slipped beneath the covers, sidling up next to her.

The sight of the bruises all over his body brought sadness to her heart. Steven had been the punching bag of the poltergeist, and even though the spirit was gone, the effects of its impact still lingered, most notably with Steven.

"I'm sorry," she started.

"For what?"

"For everything that happened the last couple days."

Steven shook his head. "Sweetie, it wasn't your fault."

"I know, but I could witness it all. The snide comments, the rude remarks, what I said about what kind of father you'd be." She studied her fingernails, ashamed at the words that had come out of her mouth. Even if they weren't her own. Swallowing the lump in her throat, she met his eyes and added, "For what it's worth, I think you're going to be a great father."

He smiled. "Thanks. I know it wasn't you."

"You know *now*," she said. "But when I said that you didn't know."

"I had an inkling."

"Still. I don't like it that I said those things." She sighed. "I just feel like everything that *I* was doing should've been preventable."

He wrapped his arm around her. "Don't put that on yourself. Clarence said you had no control."

"Did Clarence know that I was a witch?"

"I…" He paused as he thought about it. "I'm not sure. But what difference does that make?"

"As as witch I should've been able to fight off the possession more."

"But you're also pregnant."

"So that means I'm incapable of doing *anything*?"

Neither of them spoke for a moment.

Finally, Samantha said, "I just feel guilty that you have all these bruises and the nosebleeds and everything, and it was me who had the problem."

"A problem you had no control over," he said. "And I'm fine. I'm just a little stiff. I'll be okay. I was more worried about you and the baby. I'm so glad the two of you are okay." He put his hand on her belly and leaned over to kiss her.

It felt good to be in his arms again. She felt safe and cared for. But something still nagged at her. It had been on her mind for a long time, but it was especially present after the events of the last couple days.

What if something happens to the baby? What if she's unable to stop *that*? What if the baby grows up in fear? Or sees something bad happen to her?

She wanted her baby to feel safe and cared for too. She wanted him or her to not have to worry about their family being ripped apart. She wanted them to be well-prepared to take on whatever might come, which would require Samantha to train him or her as a witch. But if Steven didn't even know that their child would be a witch…

"Someone else is awake," Steven said with a smile. He looked down at his hand on her belly. "The baby just kicked."

"They're probably hungry," she said. "I haven't eaten since the shower."

"You should eat then. That'll help you get some strength. Want me to keep you company in the kitchen?"

She shook her head. "I'll be okay, thanks. Right now, I'm content just the way we are."

And that was the truth. She had a lot to worry about. A lot to think about. And a lot of people she cared for. But that's what it meant to be a wife and a mother. In the meantime, she needed to be able to live in the moment. And right here, sitting with her husband, feeling their baby kick in her belly, it was a very good moment to soak up for a bit.

CHAPTER 40

The bright side about clearing up a magical crisis on a Saturday meant that there was still Sunday to lay around and relax before the work week started. And Monday mornings actually meant something to Kathy, now that she had a full-time job.

She brought in a cup of tea for her sister, who was just waking up from yet another nap on the couch. It was her second nap of the day, the first having been just after breakfast.

"You feeling any better?" Kathy asked as she passed off the cup.

Samantha wrapped her hands around the mug, warming herself. "I feel fine—very alert right now. But when a crash comes, it comes hard. Tomorrow's going to be rough at work."

"So take a day off."

"No can do. I'm saving all my extra days off for an extended maternity leave. It's coming up soon."

"How long will you be off?"

"I'm due at the end of December, so I'm planning on being out until the end of March. My tentative return date is April 2nd, or whatever that Monday is." She took a sip of her tea. "Only half of that is paid for by work through a maternity leave, the other half will have to be both my saved up sick days and unpaid leave."

"Are you guys going to be able to swing that if it's unpaid?"

"It works out so it's only, like, a month of not having a paycheck," Samantha said. "Besides, we'll have your income for the mortgage, right?"

Kathy took a sip of her tea and remained quiet.

"Don't tell me you're quitting this job too," Samantha said.

"No, I'm not quitting. I was just thinking…"

"About?"

"Well, the baby will be here soon."

Samantha rubbed her belly. "Only two more months. I can't wait. I'm so tired of being pregnant."

Kathy smiled. "The baby's going to need a lot of room."

"We have the nursery set up. Well, mostly. You guys kind of just dropped everything yesterday when I was sleeping, which isn't what I wanted, but there were unforeseen circumstances. I'll let it slide." She grinned to show she was kidding. "Anyway, go on."

"The nursery will be fine, but you guys are going to be a family. And this big house of ours seems like it's getting smaller and smaller."

Samantha finished another sip of her tea. "We've had more people in this house before. We'll manage."

Kathy smiled, remembering faintly their grandparents living in what was now Samantha's room before they passed away. Their parents were in Kathy's room now and Samantha was in what was becoming the new baby's nursery. Kathy had been in a crib with her parents until they moved her in with Samantha. But they only shared that tiny room for a little while before their grandparents passed away, causing all sorts of rearranging of bedrooms.

It had been a tight fit with four adults and two kids, but from what little Kathy could remember, she loved having a full house all the time. But things were different now that she was one of the adults. They didn't have the third generation still living with them, like they did when they were younger.

"Well, I've been thinking," Kathy went on. "I know Steven has wanted you guys to get your own space. I mean, we wouldn't have had to perform an exorcism on you if you hadn't been looking at houses in the first place."

Samantha shook her head, tears welling up in her eyes. "Don't think that we're pushing you out."

"You're not," Kathy said. "I know that. But you guys need your own space as a family. Which means that I'm going to seriously start looking for an apartment of my own to move out."

"No, you don't have to go!" Samantha set her mug down and wiped at her eyes. "I'm going to need your help with the baby."

"And you'll have it," Kathy said, brushing away her own tears. "But I think it's time for me to be on my own. I have this great job now. And I'm only a year younger than you."

"What does that mean?"

"Well, look where you are in life compared to me."

"Life isn't a competition, Kathy."

"True, but when am I going to stop acting like a little kid? Maybe this is why I have a hard time keeping a guy around. Maybe I don't take myself seriously, so why would anyone else?"

"This last one was scared away by the demonic spirit erupting from your sister," Samantha said with a tearful chuckle. "So that one's on me."

"Sure, take the blame for Jeff," Kathy said. "I only went on one date with him!"

"You'll find someone else. How is he?"

Kathy shrugged. "I don't know. He won't return my calls."

Samantha made a face. "I'm sorry."

"It's okay. But in the future, I think it'll be easier to find—

and keep—a boyfriend if I don't have a screaming baby in the next room to kill the romance. That means getting my own place."

Samantha gave her a sad smile.

"I'll be over all the time," Kathy assured her. "I'm going to want to see this baby!"

"So you're really going, then?"

"It's time."

"I'm going to miss you."

Kathy got up and plopped on the couch beside her sister. She wrapped her in a tight hug. "I'm going to miss you too! But this isn't the end. It's just a different chapter in my life. In *our* lives. Moving out is what *normal* people do."

"We're not normal."

"We can pretend to be."

It was a change that Kathy was actually excited for. It felt right. At no fault to Samantha, Kathy had kind of been living in her sister's shadow for a long time. This move would help her see herself as her own person. It would help her become who she really was.

"Besides," Kathy added when they pulled apart. "If I want to, I can always move back in here, right?"

Not all enemies have magic.

At a dinner with her new neighbors, Samantha gets a weird vibe from their son, Dennis, who seems too interested in her and her sister and the strange things often happening at their house. That worry gets pushed aside, however, when Samantha goes into labor and rushes off to the hospital to have the baby.

Meanwhile, Dennis continues his own investigation into the sisters, tracking down people from their past who have come into close contact with them and their strangeness.

When Dennis shows up at the hospital and starts asking questions about the sisters that they believe have a malicious end, Kathy tracks him down before he has a chance to do any harm to them or Samantha's unborn baby.

Witch Hunter is the tenth book in the Coven series, which serves as a prequel to the Under the Moon series.

WITCH HUNTER

COVEN: BOOK 10

Read on for an excerpt of the next book in
the Coven series!

DAVID NETH

CHAPTER 1

- DECEMBER 1989 -

It was the first time Samantha had been in the house across the street since they had defeated the shapeshifter. The house where she and her husband had been held captive. The house that sat directly across the street from theirs, as a constant reminder of everything that had happened just over a year ago.

To be sitting and sipping tea casually on some of the same furniture that had been in the house when they had been abducted was an irony that didn't slip her mind.

"Thanks again for having us over, Mr. Kors," she said to her neighbor. The new neighbors had moved in a little more than a year ago, not too long after the police had finished up their investigation.

"It's good that we finally got to do this," he said. "And call me

Gerald. We're neighbors, not colleagues." He reached in his pocket for his cigarettes and offered one to Steven.

Samantha's husband declined with a shake of his head, then motioned to his wife and said to Gerald, "Would you mind not smoking in front of Samantha? We don't want anything to hurt the baby."

"Huh?" Gerald studied them, then put the pack back in his chest pocket. "Oh. Oh, sure. How much longer do you have?"

"Hopefully not much." Samantha rubbed her belly. She was grateful for the cold weather and the fact that she could better hide her size under layers of sweaters. Not that she really needed them with the heat from the baby. "I'm due at the end of the month."

Pressing both hands against the arms of his chair, the old man swung forward once before rocking back and launching himself to his feet on the second try. He let out a groan as he stood straight. "That would be why Nancy was so insistent on inviting the two of you over. She wanted the both of you to enjoy a night before the baby came." He walked over to the credenza built into the wall. "You want a drink, Steven? To celebrate."

Steven cast a sidelong look at his wife before answering. "Um…sure."

Samantha knew that her husband was only accepting the drink because he had denied Gerald his cigarettes. For better or worse, her husband was a peacekeeper.

"What do you want? I've got scotch, whiskey, gin. You name

it, I can mix it."

"Um…whiskey, I guess."

Gerald smiled and reached for a glass bottle.

"Does Nancy need any help in the kitchen?" Samantha hated sitting and chitchatting while the elderly woman worked on the meal they were all about to enjoy. Judging by the savory scents wafting from around the corner, they were in for a treat.

"Nah, she's okay." Mr. Kors handed Steven a highball glass filled to the brim with the brown liquid. "If she needs something, she'll holler. She's already had me set the table real nice for you folks." He retook his seat and then raised it in the air in a toast. "To you two on this new parenting journey."

Steven obliged, raising his glass and then bringing it to his lips for a sip. Samantha covered her mouth as she watched, trying to hide the grin as she saw the displeasure clear on her husband's face. He wasn't much of a drinker, and when it did it certainly wasn't hard liquor.

The conversation fell into silence as Gerald enjoyed his drink. Steven took a few more sips and then set it on the table beside him.

Samantha looked around and admired the Christmas tree that sat in the front window. She had seen it from her house across the street, but it was more impressive in person. It shone bright with white lights and handmade ornaments made of paper, cardboard, and clay. She smiled, recognizing what exactly that meant. Someday she'd have a collection of crafts that her own child would make for her too.

"How do you like living here?" Steven asked.

"It's nice," Gerald said. "Quiet street. Nice neighbors. Even if it's an old house, it's not too bad. Keeps me young, going around and fixing everything that's wrong."

"Everything's beautiful." Samantha looked around at the garland hung around the cased doorways and the Christmas cards taped to the doorframe leading to the kitchen.

"To be honest, I think the previous owners did a lot of renovation work—well, two owners ago, I guess. The last ones were a bit—you know—loony."

Samantha looked down at her tea and smirked. She knew exactly how *loony* they had been.

"So how did that work?" Steven asked. "With the last owners, I mean."

"How did what work?"

"Well, they were…*killed*, right?"

Gerald nodded. "That's right."

"So how did you and your wife end up buying it?"

"Ah," the old man said with a nod and a smile. "You see, what happened here made a bit of a splash in the news—I can only imagine what you two thought, living just across the street. Maybe I should be asking *you* the questions."

Samantha hoped he wouldn't. She wasn't sure what lie she could come up with that would fit in with the story he had been told by the realtor who sold him the house.

"The house wasn't on the market long," Steven said.

Gerald shook his head. "No, it wasn't. But long enough for the realtor to start to get worried. See, she knew about the bodies they had found in the basement—and the blood up in the bedroom. She was eager to sell this place to get it off her caseload. And for the three weeks that it was listed, this place had no one coming to see it. Not a single person. From what I understand, the few people who were interested were turned away when they found out that several people had been murdered—and chopped up—in this place. So when Nancy and I saw it, we were able to negotiate a great deal."

"And the murders don't bother you?" Samantha asked.

He shrugged. "It's in the past. No murderers live here now. And the police brought a team in that cleaned everything up for us. This place was spotless when we bought it!"

"But isn't your master bedroom where one of the murders happened?" Steven asked. "The news said they found blood on the wallpaper."

Gerald made a face and shook his head. "Didn't like that wallpaper anyway. We ripped it out, put up new stuff that Nancy picked out. Some flowers or shit, I don't know. Don't care, either. I just sleep in there—and occasionally, other stuff."

Samantha raised her eyebrows at that comment and quickly thought of something to change the subject. "Well, you wouldn't be able to tell based on the way everything looks now. It's a very nice and inviting home."

Gerald smiled and opened his mouth to reply, but the front door creaked as it opened. Snowy, cold air hit them as a young man stepped into the house.

"Hey Dad," he said.

Gerald stared in surprise. "Dennis?"

CHAPTER 2

Bon Jovi blared from the speakers as Kathy leaned in close to hear her friend Trisha speak over the music.

"He's looking right at you!" Trisha tilted her chin to the guy across the bar who had been staring in Kathy's direction for the last ten minutes.

Kathy glanced back at him and smiled. He *was* cute.

"Don't tell me you haven't noticed him," Trisha said.

"Of course I've noticed him, but I still don't *know* him." The last thing Kathy wanted—or needed—was to get involved with someone. She was still a little nervous about even trying to date someone after she had completely made herself look like a freak with her last date, Jeff. And that's not to mention her on-again, off-again relationship with Jeremy, which was now definitely *off*.

She needed to be single for a little while.

At least until someone special came around.

"So go over there and *get* to know him!" Trisha said. "Take him upstairs for a private chat."

Kathy shook her head. "You know I'm not here for that."

"Isn't that why you moved out? To be able to do whatever you want? Your sister isn't here. Let yourself live a little!"

That was true. Kathy's apartment was just above the bar—and surprisingly looked very similar to the one she had experienced during her illusion at the hands of the trickster she and Samantha had faced back in May.

Kathy had been out on her own for about a month now and she had been playing it safe ever since, as if she were still under the watchful eye of her big sister. First her excuse was that she wanted to get settled into her new place. Then it was that she wanted to make sure her finances were in order before she let herself have any sort of fun that required spending money. And now it was…what?

"Look, the last few times we've gone out, you've had a problem with every single guy I've found for you," Trisha said. "How do you expect me to be a wingwoman when you won't even take my leads?"

She looked over at her friend and sighed, not that anyone could hear it over the noise of the bar. "Okay fine. I'll go ask him his name and see if he makes any moves after that. But if things get awkward—or weird—I'm out of there!"

"And I'll be here to help fend him off if need be. Just go and give this guy a chance!"

With butterflies in her belly—when was the last time she was nervous about talking to a guy?—Kathy slipped off the barstool and crossed the room. She only made it halfway before a different guy caught her eye.

Michael.

Jeremy's friend.

"Kathy?" he asked, wide-eyed with surprise.

"Hey!" Very naturally, they moved in for a hug that lasted longer than Kathy had expected. Not that she was complaining about that. She got along great with Michael, even if he had always just been Jeremy's friend to her. She hadn't seen him since May when she and Jeremy had broken up.

When they pulled apart, both of them smiled wide at each other, but neither knew what to say. Kathy *wanted* a conversation to suddenly spring up, but she couldn't think of a good enough thing to say to warrant that kind of discourse.

"How—"

"So—"

They both started talking and stopped when they realized they were about to talk over each other.

"Sorry," he said. "You go."

She shook her head. "No, it's okay. You can go." The best thing she could come up was to ask how he'd been. Small Talk 101. Lame.

"So Jeremy's been doing okay," he said.

"Yeah?" Her voice carried no interest, even though she *was* interested in how her ex was doing without her.

"Not great," he added. "Just okay."

"Is he still drinking?" She noted the irony. Asking the question while they stood in the middle of a bar; a few drinks already working their way into her bloodstream.

Michael pursed his lips and nodded. "Yeah, he is. Quite a bit. I'm actually moving out because things between me and him just aren't the same since college. I'm getting out of that party phase and he still seems locked in it. And I know it's only depression, but he refuses to even acknowledge it, which is so frustrating. Wow."

"What?"

"I sound like I'm his wife or something," he said with a chuckle.

She smiled, glad that he had successfully lightened the mood.

"I just don't want to watch him spiral anymore," Michael said. "And it's time I grew up and got my own place anyway."

"Well, I'm happy for you. Actually, I just moved out on my own last month."

His eyebrows raised. "You did? I didn't think you'd ever move out of that house!"

"With the baby coming soon and Samantha and Steven coming up on their first anniversary, I thought it was a good time to be on my own too." She pointed to the ceiling. "It's right upstairs."

"Is this your new hangout then?"

Her apartment—and the bar—were at the southeastern end of downtown, by the railroad tracks. Far away from the watering holes in Lawrence Park or the ones downtown that were often filled with college students from Gannon University—the crowds that she used to be drawn to not that long ago.

Kathy shrugged. "Guess so. I've only been here a handful of times, but I like it."

She looked past Michael and saw the guy she had been on her way to talk to. He was now nursing his drink, peeling the label off his bottle and no longer looking in her direction. She looked back at Trisha, who was deep in conversation with a man seated beside her at the bar.

"Looking for someone?" Michael asked.

She turned back to him. "Just checking on my friend. She seems to be occupied. Do you want to go upstairs so we could talk easier? This place is a little too noisy for me."

He smiled. "Sure. I'd love that."

CHAPTER 3

Nancy Kors emerged from the kitchen and her face immediately lit up, nearly as much as her Christmas tree.

"Dennis! What a surprise!" the woman shrieked as she wrapped her arms tightly around her son.

After his mother let him go, the newcomer moved on to hug Gerald. Samantha and Steven looked at each other, unsure of what to do. Samantha felt like they were suddenly crashing an intimate family moment.

"Come on in!" Nancy waved him forward. "Let me take your coat. Gerald, dear, take his bag!"

While she pulled Dennis's jacket off of him, her husband took the duffel bag out of his hands.

"What are you doing here?" Gerald asked. "I thought you were at sea?"

"I was able to get an early leave." He turned to look at Samantha and Steven and asked, "I'm not interrupting anything, am I?"

Samantha put up her hand and shook her head with a polite smile. "Not at all."

"Don't worry about it," Steven added.

Gerald stepped back and stretched his arm out toward Samantha and Steven, who both rose. "I'd like you to meet our neighbors, the Harpers. This is Steven and his wife, Samantha."

Dennis shook both of their hands as polite pleasantries were exchanged.

"We were all just about to sit down to dinner," Nancy said. She looked to their guests. "You wouldn't mind if Dennis joined us, would you?"

"Mom, I don't want to impose or anything—"

"Really, it's no bother," Samantha said. "He's your son. Of course you want to see him. Maybe we should actually head home so you can—"

"No, you don't have to go and do that," Gerald said. "Sit! Stay a while! We can all get to know each other."

"It's just that Dennis is in the Navy and we don't get to see him very often." Nancy reached up and patted her son's cheek and beamed with delight.

"When the opportunity to come home early came up, I

knew I had to take it to surprise you guys as an early Christmas present," Dennis said.

Nancy wrapped her arm around his waist. "And what a wonderful surprise this is!" From the kitchen, the oven timer dinged. "Oh shoot. I need to go take the lasagna out of the oven. I'll be right back!"

After she disappeared into the kitchen, the room turned awkward again.

"Let's take a seat," Gerald suggested as he plopped back into his recliner.

Samantha and Steven both retook their seats while Dennis opted for the loveseat in the corner.

"So Dennis, you're in the Navy, huh?" Steven started.

"Yes, sir."

"I have a friend who's in the Navy. He was the best man at our wedding."

"What ship is he stationed on?"

"The *Constellation*?" Steven looked to Samantha for confirmation. She could only vaguely remember Robert mentioning what ship he was on. All she knew was that he was out in southern California now.

Dennis nodded with recognition. "Ah, so he's out of San Diego."

"Yeah, I think so."

"I'm on the *South Carolina*, out of Norfolk."

"How often are you actually out on the water?"

As Steven and Dennis continued their conversation, Gerald turned to Samantha and said, "I've noticed it was pretty dark across the street at your house. No lights again this year?"

She shook her head. "No. Christmas isn't really our thing."

"You had a wreath out last year. And some candles in the windows. Looked nice."

"That was my sister. She really loves the commercialism of Christmas, but she's out on her own now so the house is just mine and Steven's."

"So no lights?"

She shook her head. "Not this year, no."

"Are you Jewish?"

"No, I'm not," she said with a chuckle. Every time someone heard that she didn't celebrate Christmas, they immediately assumed that she was Jewish.

"So then what do you believe in?"

The question was brusque, but Samantha could tell he didn't mean anything by it. Still, it was an uncomfortable topic and one that she wished to brush off without any further question.

"Well, in December we sometimes celebrate the winter solstice."

Gerald narrowed his eyes. "What does that mean?"

"The shortest day of the year. The changing of seasons. It's more of a spiritual thing for us. Although, in the past, my sister has convinced me to get a tree and participate in *some* Christmas traditions. It's hard not to. I love gingerbread!"

The joke was her attempt to lighten the mood and shift the conversation away, but instead her words were noted by Dennis.

"You don't believe in God?"

Just as to-the-point as his father…

Samantha shifted in her seat. "Um…well…"

"My wife isn't a Christian," Steven said in her defense.

Dennis turned to Steven. "But you are?"

He shrugged. "It's how I was raised."

"And you're okay with throwing out your religion for her?"

"Just because we have some differences doesn't mean I can't respect what she believes," Steven countered.

Dennis shook his head. "I just don't see how that's going to work long-term."

"Uh…" Gerald cut in loudly, trying to diffuse the growing tension. "Samantha, are you going to do anymore Christmas traditions when the baby comes?"

She turned to her husband, again uncomfortable by the spotlight she was suddenly under. "Well, Steven and I haven't really discussed it yet…"

"Wait, you're having a *baby*?" Dennis asked, wide-eyed.

Nancy appeared in the doorway and cheerfully announced, "Dinner's ready!"

Relief washed over Samantha as they all rose and moved to the dining room.

Dinner was going to be hell.

TO READ THE REST OF **WITCH HUNTER**, ORDER YOUR COPY AT DAVIDNETHBOOKS.COM/COVEN

FIND ALL THE BOOKS IN THE COVEN SERIES!

PICK UP THE FIRST BOOK IN THE UNDER THE MOON SERIES!

Kathy and her sister, Samantha, have always been a team. Throughout their time as witches, they've taken out more than their share of bad guys. But after Kathy meets Will, who she learns is a demonic Dark Knight, her loyalties begin to change.

Meanwhile, Samantha doesn't trust Will or his intentions. Still, Kathy can't help but feel tempted by the dark side as she falls deeper in love with Will. Crossing over would give Kathy the freedom to do whatever she wanted with her magic. No rules. No limitations. It would also mean breaking the bond she has always shared with her sister, who has made it clear that she wants nothing to do with the dark side.

When Will proposes they take over the underworld, Kathy loves the idea of having power. But it also leaves her with a choice that will change her life: abandon her family and the life she has always known, or give up the love of her life forever.

MORE BY THE AUTHOR

To find more books by the author, visit
DavidNethBooks.com/Books

* * *

Subscribe to his newsletter to be the first to know of new
releases and special deals!
DavidNethBooks.com/Newsletter

* * *

**If you enjoyed the book, please consider leaving a
review on Goodreads or the retailer you bought it from.**
Reviews help potential readers determine whether
they'll enjoy a book, so any comments on what you
thought of the story would be very helpful!

ABOUT THE AUTHOR

David Neth is the author of the Coven series, the Under the Moon series, Heat series, the Fuse series, and other stories. He lives in Batavia, NY, where he dreams of a successful publishing career and opening his own bookstore.

Also writes small town romance as D. Allen.

www.DavidNethBooks.com

www.facebook.com/DavidNethBooks